Praise for *Revolution*

Aubin has done it again! *Revolution: The Ship Series Book Two* is a darker and deeper sequel to *Landfall* filled with heart, humor, and page-turning adventure. Aubin takes us into the hidden workings of The Ship and the restless strata of civilians ripe for rebellion. *Revolution* continues the thrilling ride of *The Ship* series with new threats, new allies, and surprises around every corner.

- Owen Egerton, author of *Everyone Says That at the End of the World*

REVOLUTION

THE SHIP SERIES // BOOK TWO

JERRY AUBIN

For any information, please contact zax@theshipseries.com.

The main text of this book was set in Georgia.
The chapter title text was set in Avenir.

Lekanyane Publishing
Austin // Amsterdam // Cape Town // Sydney // Christchurch

ISBN 978-0-9970708-3-5 (pbk)
ISBN 978-0-9970708-2-8 (ebk)

For K, P, W, and Q.

CHAPTER ONE
WHAT THE HELL WERE YOU THINKING, ZAX?   1

CHAPTER TWO
JUST PROTECTING THE SHIP ONE PIPE FULL OF SEWAGE AT A TIME.   9

CHAPTER THREE
THEY GET ALL THE BENEFIT AND WE BEAR ALL THE COST.   15

CHAPTER FOUR
OUCH!   23

CHAPTER FIVE
YOU EAT IT.   33

CHAPTER SIX
WHY THE APPLE?   41

CHAPTER SEVEN
HELLO, ZAX.   47

CHAPTER EIGHT
PRETTY EFFECTIVE, IF I DO SAY SO MYSELF.   53

CHAPTER NINE
WE KNOW THEY ARE OUT THERE SOMEWHERE.   61

CHAPTER TEN
YOU CAN HELP THEM.   71

CHAPTER ELEVEN
I AGREE WITH ALERON.   79

CHAPTER TWELVE
GIVE ME THE BLASTER!   85

CHAPTER THIRTEEN
WE HAVE TO DELIVER A MESSAGE.   91

CHAPTER FOURTEEN
WHY DID YOU DO THAT?   99

CHAPTER FIFTEEN
WITH ALL DUE RESPECT, SIR, WE SHOULDN'T SPLIT UP.   105

CHAPTER SIXTEEN
WHERE ARE WE?   111

CHAPTER SEVENTEEN
IT WAS DELICIOUS, SIR.   117

CHAPTER EIGHTEEN
YOU CAN THANK CAPTAIN CLUELESS OVER THERE.   123

CHAPTER NINETEEN
WE CAN PRETEND ALL OF THAT SILLINESS NEVER HAPPENED.   131

CHAPTER TWENTY
WE CAN'T LET YOU HAVE ALL THE FUN TODAY.   137

CHAPTER TWENTY-ONE
I KNOW WHERE ONE IS.   145

CHAPTER TWENTY-TWO
HE WILL BE AWAKE IN THIRTY MINS.   151

CHAPTER TWENTY-THREE
WHY ARE YOU NICE TO ME?   161

CHAPTER TWENTY-FOUR
PERMISSION TO SPEAK FREELY, SIR?   167

CHAPTER TWENTY-FIVE
PEACE IS AT HAND.   175

CHAPTER TWENTY-SIX
I KNOW EXACTLY WHAT I'M DOING.   183

CHAPTER TWENTY-SEVEN
I'LL CARRY THE BOY.   189

CHAPTER TWENTY-EIGHT
EVERYONE TAKE A DEEP BREATH.   197

CHAPTER TWENTY-NINE
YOU NEED TO LOOK AT THE BIG PICTURE.   201

CHAPTER THIRTY
I NEED YOU OUT OF THAT SUIT, CORPORAL.   209

CHAPTER THIRTY-ONE
THE FATE OF THE SHIP IS IN YOUR HANDS RIGHT NOW.   213

CHAPTER THIRTY-TWO
DON'T LET HER GET AWAY!   219

CHAPTER THIRTY-THREE
WILL YOU ACTUALLY SHOOT THIS TIME?   225

CHAPTER THIRTY-FOUR
SHOW YOUR HANDS!   233

CHAPTER THIRTY-FIVE
LOOK WHO WE HAVE HERE.   239

CHAPTER THIRTY-SIX
THERE'S NOTHING YOU CAN DO, ZAX!   247

CHAPTER THIRTY-SEVEN
SHE'S IN FOR THE SURPRISE OF HER LIFE.   253

CHAPTER THIRTY-EIGHT
WHAT HAVE YOU DONE?   259

CHAPTER THIRTY-NINE
PLEASE OPEN THE HATCH.   265

CHAPTER FORTY
I'M MAKING GOOD ON THAT PROMISE.   273

CHAPTER FORTY-ONE
NOT THIS ALL OVER AGAIN...   281

ACKNOWLEDGMENTS   290

CHAPTER ONE

What the hell were you thinking, Zax?

An explosion flared on his viewscreen when Zax shattered the enemy spacecraft with a burst of blue ion pulses. Three more dull-gray alien orbs, each bristling with plasma cannons, maneuvered behind him and prepared to fire. He attempted to escape by accelerating his fighter straight into the heart of the expanding blast. Flying through the remnants of your opposition wasn't a recommended evasive maneuver given the likelihood of damaging your own craft, but it was the best of the bad options Zax had left for himself.

The fighter screens tinged orange from the burning wreckage of the enemy, and a sharp *crack* signaled that Zax's fighter had collided with something sizeable enough to ruin his day. Damage alarms wailed and flashed as the fighter refused to respond to his commands.

"What the hell were you thinking, Zax? You were supposed to back off and wait until Red 23 could provide cover, but instead you dove in and engaged this group all on your own. If you managed to hit that debris from a slightly different angle, we'd be part of that explosion right now!"

Kalare was not always a fan of his piloting choices, but she seemed especially pissed today. Zax often wondered whether she regretted her choice to fly with him as his Weapons System Operator. He was grateful to share the fighter with his only friend, but he sometimes fantasized about having a WSO who just shut up and let him fly however he saw fit.

"Point taken, Kalare. How bad's the damage?"

"There's a load of problems, but the biggest is secondary weapons control got totally fried. Give me another couple secs, and I will get primary weps back online and flight control stable—for now."

A different alert squawked and pulled his attention back to the threat board. Red 23 finally caught up with them but immediately came under heavy fire from the same aliens Zax managed to dodge. His disabled craft's uncontrolled inertia carried him away from the battle, so Zax was unable to do anything but watch in grim silence as the enemy overwhelmed his wingman with a rain of fiery plasma. An alien shot found its target, and Zax averted his attention from the viewscreen so he wouldn't witness the smooth silver needle of Red 23's fighter rupture into a million fragments.

A piercing tone cycled on and off and provided Zax with a moment of relief. The noise signaled that the pilot and WSO of Red 23 had not died when their fighter was destroyed. The armored Core which protected the biological matrix containing their minds had instead been ejected successfully. The Ship would deploy a Search and Rescue craft to collect the Core and their consciousnesses would be returned to their waiting bodies onboard the Ship. Zax called the Commander, Air Group using her call sign.

"Cobra—Red 23 is gone, but I've got pings showing their Core ejected successfully. We going to get any more help out here? They're relatively slow and reasonably stupid, but these aliens outnumber us by at least a hundred to one and we're getting chewed up pretty bad."

"You're damn right about how we need more help, Z. Your wingman's Core is floating uselessly and your fighter is practically toast as well—all because you couldn't manage to follow my orders and stay with him. Head back to the Ship immediately before you take any more damage and I need two SAR birds out here to collect two Cores."

Zax held his frustration in check and replied, "Aye-aye, CAG." He considered complaining to Kalare about the commander's directive but abstained knowing she'd likely use it as yet another opportunity to admonish him about his questionable piloting choices. Kalare restored flight control a short time later, and Zax turned his craft back towards the Ship.

It took 190 secs for Zax to weave his way through the clusters of enemy spacecraft and reach the leading edge where they had been thinned out and were no longer a threat. He was still a tremendous distance away from the Ship, but his augmented viewscreen allowed him to make out the craggy outlines of its massive rocky base as well as the twinkling lights from the millions of viewports which adorned the structures along its upper half. The CAG had ordered him to return, but she hadn't been explicit about how fast he needed to get there. Zax reduced his speed to five percent. If he wasn't allowed to fight, he might as well hang around and observe what he was missing.

"Kalare—can you please give me an expanded threat board?"

"Sure thing, Zax. Are you upset about being pulled from the battle? I bet you're upset about being pulled from the battle. If you were looking at the same damage readouts I'm seeing, you'd totally agree with the CAG. Besides, now we can watch what all of the other fighters are doing and learn from them. I always think it can be super useful to watch the more experienced pilots and WSOs to see how they handle situations in the middle of an engagement. Like Red 12 there. Did you see how she destroyed those four alien craft in front of her? After she did it, she inverted herself 180 degrees and *avoided their debris field altogether. She could do that because her wingman was right there with her and had kept her six clear of any trailing aliens. I think that was a pretty smooth move. Don't you agree that was a smooth move?"*

Zax was thrilled that he and Kalare were communicating at the speed of thought over their fighter's neural network. It meant any monologues would flash by in an instant as compared to how long it would take if she was physically speaking to him. He probably should be more sensitive to Kalare's feedback since they'd both be dead if their fighter was ever annihilated to the point its Core was destroyed. The odds of that happening were slim, though, so her passive-aggressive critique of his piloting rankled. He decided to let it pass and silence filled the virtual space between them rather than the sarcastic reply he had on the tip of his virtual tongue.

The threat board would look like a random maelstrom of activity to most people, but Zax had always possessed a preternatural ability to tease patterns out of chaos. After a short period of intense focus, he recognized a new threat emerging. Six of the enemy spacecraft maintained a tight formation and allowed an unending stream of their fellow pilots to sacrifice themselves as a moving shield against the Ship's fighters. The sheer number of identical fighters made it impossible for the humans in the middle of it all to pay attention to any one alien craft versus another. Since Zax watched the big picture from afar, he recognized the subtle shifting of the enemy movements which protected the six fighters and allowed them to approach the edge of the battle zone closest to the Ship.

The six alien craft moved together until they appeared as a single fighter on the threat board and accelerated en masse towards the Ship. At the same instant, all of the remaining alien craft stopped battling the human fighters around them, swiveled in the direction of the Ship, and unleashed a continuous barrage from their plasma cannons. The aliens were far enough from the Ship that even such concentrated fire wouldn't do serious damage to the vessel, but the rain of plasma bolts destroyed all of its defenders which were in the formation's path.

"Kalare—did you see what just happened there? We've got to stop that group of fighters speeding towards the Ship!"

Zax vectored his fighter towards the aliens and pushed its acceleration close to the maximum. The Ship's fighters were designed for situations just like this one. A human pilot would never survive the staggering g-forces generated during such high-speed maneuvers. With their bodies back on board the Ship, all Zax and Kalare experienced was a sensation of movement carefully calibrated to provide their minds with a "feel" for what was physically happening with their fighter.

The human defensive force destroyed aliens at an even faster pace since they were no longer shooting back, but there were still so many enemy spacecraft providing cover with their plasma cannons that the resultant wall of fire was nearly impenetrable. Zax pointed his fighter towards the shower of plasma bolts without a moment's hesitation.

It required every bit of Zax's skill to thread his fighter through a series of gaps in the aliens' covering fire, but he successfully made his way until the six-craft formation was within secs of weapons range. Five alien fighters had attached themselves to one craft in the middle to form a single unit. Kalare was preparing a full spread of ion blasts targeted at the center of the formation when an alien plasma round connected with their fighter. Zax had almost dodged it like so many before, but he misjudged its trajectory by the smallest fraction and suffered a glancing blow. Once again, alarms flashed and wailed within his fighter.

"Zax—we've lost primary weapons control! We can't shoot at them so there isn't anything we can do. Get out of here!"

"We've got to do something—no one else can stop them before they get within range of the Ship! We've got to ram them!"

The potential consequence of that action hung in the silence between the two of them for what felt like an eternity although it was only millisecs. Zax addressed it directly.

"We've always been told how well-armored our Cores are. I guess this is a chance to put it to the test. If ours gets destroyed and we die, at least the Crew will send our bodies into space together. We'll float forever with each other for company."

Kalare was silent for a long moment before she replied.

"OK. You're right. Do it."

Zax triggered his fighter's emergency acceleration. It would deplete his fuel within secs, but it was sufficient to reach the alien formation. The enemy fighters loomed larger and larger as Zax closed the gap from behind. The formation attempted to evade at the last moment, but he had anticipated their response and matched their vector change instantaneously.

There was a blinding light from the explosion. The physical sensations of the violent impact were not transferred to Zax's mind, so he experienced the destruction visually as a slow motion rending of the spacecraft into a constellation of debris. A sensation of weightlessness signaled that the fighter's Core had been successfully ejected and was floating freely in space as the lifeboat for his and Kalare's minds.

"We did it!"

Zax exulted in their success for a fraction of a sec. Then a secondary explosion breached the Core and expelled the fragile biological matrix which contained his and Kalare's minds into the unforgiving vacuum of space.

CHAPTER TWO

Just protecting the Ship one pipe full

of sewage at a time.

"Wow, Zax!" Kalare gasped for breath. Sweat had formed on her brow and slicked the jet-black hair which framed her face. The gold flecks in her blue eyes shimmered even in the dull glow of the mess hall lighting. "What a ride! That was awesome!"

Zax grinned from ear to ear. He had worked on the simulator for months and was thrilled to see its physical effect on Kalare. His own heartrate was maxed out and he was panting as well, so it was clear their nervous systems were fully engaged. This had been the last hurdle in his programming efforts, and he appeared to have cleared it with room to spare.

Zax gazed around. The cavernous mess hall had emptied out substantially. The two of them were so immersed in the simulation they appeared to have missed most of the breakfast period. He appreciated how strange they must have looked sitting there, breathing hard with their eyes closed to focus on the simulation shared across their neural Plugs, but ultimately he couldn't care less. Kalare continued.

"It's just about as good as the ones we use in the Pilot Academy! Oops! I'm sorry, Zax—I did it again. I hate how I keep talking about my training. It must be so hard for you to hear."

"It's OK. It really doesn't bother me that much."

Zax was being only partially truthful. He didn't mind hearing all of Kalare's stories about the ins and outs of pilot training. They helped him stay focused on finding a path that would get his career out of the toilet and back on track. What bothered him immensely, however, was the look she gave him *every—single—time* she realized she was in the middle of another one. He didn't need her pity and once again attempted to dispel any reason for her to think otherwise.

"Working in Waste Systems could be a lot worse. The woman I report to doesn't care what I do all day as long as the machines keep running and I stay out of her hair. The civilians do most of the real work, so I usually spend my shifts volunteering for whatever extra credit assignments I can find to rebuild my Leaderboard ranking. I even manage to find time to work on stuff that interests me—like this sim.

"And I *really* don't mind hearing about the Pilot Academy. I don't think I would have worried as much about the physical effects of my simulator if I hadn't seen the look on your face whenever you talked about any of the training exercises you've been through."

"I'll say it again then, your simulation is as good as the ones in the Pilot Academy!" Kalare paused for a sec to close her eyes and check her Plug. "Hey— it's getting late and I should get going. What's on your schedule today?"

"Oh you know—nothing much. Just protecting the Ship one pipe full of sewage at a time. How about you?"

Kalare rewarded Zax with one of her big, beaming smiles in response to his joke. "I actually don't know. I've got a shift in Flight Ops in a few mins, but the Boss said something about the two of us going on a field trip. I have no idea what that might mean."

Zax couldn't prevent himself from wincing ever so slightly. He didn't mind hearing about Kalare's pilot training, but mentions of the Flight Boss were something else entirely. It still felt like only yesterday that his decision to defy the second most powerful officer on board and attempt to expose the man's actions had sent Zax's career into a near-death spiral.

Kalare picked up on Zax's discomfort. "I'm sorry about bringing up the Boss, Zax, but you've just got to get over it already."

"Get over it? Get over it? You had 'gotten over' Flight and wanted to join the Marines. Do you remember that? But somehow a year later you've become more focused on your career than you ever were before. I wanted the Boss's mentorship *more than anything* back when you were rolling dice to pick your next assignment. Knowing I did the right thing doesn't make it any easier to pretend I'm not hurt when I see my friend enjoying a prime spot that could have also been mine." Zax paused for a sec. "Wow— it's hard to believe it's been a year already. I suppose time flies after you kill your career."

The compassion in Kalare's eyes was plain to see even as her voice revealed plenty of frustration. "I'm sorry, Zax, but you can't honestly believe I would still have anything to do with the Boss if I thought there was any truth to your accusations. Don't *you remember* how *we decided* I would accept his mentorship so I could stick close to him and see what I could learn about his role in Mikedo's death? Isn't it reasonable that I've determined you were wrong and he had nothing to do with it after all? Yes—I care about becoming a pilot more now that I've had a taste of it, but you seem to be suggesting that I'm disagreeing with your beliefs about the Boss purely out of self-interest. That hurts too. I'm sorry you trashed your career chasing your suspicions, but at some point you have to be willing to accept they were wrong."

Hearing Mikedo's name had the predictable effect on Zax. Even a year after the young officer's death, he still got weepy thinking about her. He knew her for only a short time, but she changed his outlook on life forever during those intense few weeks when she led the training contest for the Boss's mentorship.

Without Mikedo's influence he would probably still be near the top of the Leaderboard experiencing firsthand the pilot training he now only glimpsed through Kalare's eyes, although he'd have been doing it entirely on his own. Mikedo cracked open his shell and forced not only herself but also Kalare inside. Even if they couldn't see eye to eye about the Boss, Kalare was still the only person who truly cared about Zax, and he remained grateful for her friendship.

While Zax took a moment to get his emotions in check, the morning newsvid began to blare out of the screens around the mess hall. He looked up and saw the announcer superimposed over an image of a burned out Tube junction.

"The recent spate of destruction and bloodshed continues with a 300th consecutive day of violent unrest among the civilian population. In addition to the hundreds of agitators justifiably killed by Marines for damaging the Ship and harming our Crew, there have been almost 15,000 civilians Culled over the past year for their role in these heinous riots. Generations of civilians have been honorably

protected by our brave Crew for millennia and yet for some unknown reason a faction has turned their backs on that proud history and threaten our peaceful existence together. Let's go down to the scene of today's riot for more details about this latest bout of senseless ruination."

Zax latched on to the newsvid story and diverted their conversation away from yet another debate about the Boss. "Well, I hope your field trip doesn't get impacted by this latest disturbance. Every day there's a different area of the Ship we're supposed to avoid. It seems whenever the Marines get one riot mopped up, another two pop up to take its place."

"I know! It's gotten so crazy the Boss doesn't travel anywhere on his own anymore. The other day when he brought me to lunch at the Omega's mess hall, we were shadowed by six Marine guards!"

"Well...I'm glad to hear you'll be safe wherever you go with him," Zax said with as much faux lightheartedness as he could muster. "I can't imagine any civilians stupid enough to try anything when a half-dozen Marines are around!"

Kalare and Zax shared a laugh and gathered their trays for disposal as they stood to leave. Zax grabbed an apple off the pile on the counter and slipped it into his pocket (ten demerits) as they departed the mess hall and went their separate ways.

CHAPTER THREE

They get all the benefit and we bear all the cost.

Zax had two tasks on his agenda before he was due in Waste Systems. He was scheduled for advanced Plug training later in the morning, but before then had to lead a lesson for a group of eleven-year-old cadets from Gamma Cadre. Teaching used to be one of his favorite activities because the younger cadets had eagerly devoured his tales about Flight Ops. Zax's tumble down the Leaderboard, though, drastically reduced the Gammas' interest in his stories. They still had to defer to his position above them in the Ship's hierarchy and his power to influence their rankings via the assessment of credits and demerits, but the group's dwindling respect had become increasingly noticeable over the last year.

At least they would move along to another instructor soon. This cohort of students had witnessed Zax's descent from Flight Ops to Waste Systems, but the next would only ever know him as the loser at the bottom of the Leaderboard they had gotten stuck with. Never having respect in the first place struck him as a more palatable prospect than losing it.

The training compartment buzzed with nervous energy. The words "civilians" and "riot" and "Tube" could be picked out repeatedly from the pockets of chatter around the room. Zax was supposed to provide the Gammas a primer on the inner workings of the Ship's gravity generation system, but he decided to start instead with a discussion of the civilian situation given it was a topic he had more than a passing familiarity with.

The newsvid announcer had professed ignorance about the rationale for the non-stop civilian unrest, but Zax was certain it traced back to his actions in Flight Ops a year earlier. Before she died, Mikedo had convinced him their discovery of a mysterious spacecraft from Earth might spark a revolution. She believed evidence proving the Ship was not the sole remnant of humanity would radically destabilize an already teetering society built upon 5,000 years of that mythos. Between what he saw for himself after Mikedo's death and what he learned from her final message to him, Zax had recognized the power of their shared secret and concluded the only way to prevent himself and Kalare from suffering the same fate was to expose it.

Zax shocked the Flight Ops staff with Mikedo's video of the human spacecraft during his confrontation with the Boss a year ago. The same clash where he announced one of the Omegas had killed her to hide that evidence. The first riot occurred scant days later and Zax was confident word of the video had spread throughout the Ship and ultimately triggered the violence. Of course, Zax couldn't share all of those juicy details with the Gammas, but he was curious to hear their perspectives.

"Cadets—what's with all of the commotion? What are you all so excited about?"

Zax acknowledged the raised hand of a girl sitting in the front row of the compartment.

"Sir, didn't you watch the morning newsvid? There was another civilian riot and this one destroyed a Tube junction a group of us just used the other day."

"Interesting. Who can tell me why the civilians keep forcing us to deal with all of this violence?"

"Because they're idiots," said a boy towards the back of the class.

"That is the obvious root cause, but ten demerits for speaking without raising your hand." Zax glared at the boy, but the Gamma smirked back at him. He was one of the cadets who had become increasingly brazen with his disrespect. "Does anyone have anything more insightful to offer as to why the civilians have been rioting for the past year?"

Zax looked around the room, but all of the hands remained down. He let everyone wallow in the uncomfortable silence for a min until finally the same girl who originally spoke raised her hand again.

"I don't think anyone really knows why this has been going on for so long, sir. I just know it doesn't make any sense to me. I mean, the Crew has spent thousands of years defending the civilians from all manner of alien attacks, right? I don't understand why they can't appreciate how many of us have died keeping the Ship safe during our Mission. I've heard some Crew say we should just put all of them into cryostorage and be done with it. That's never seemed like the right answer to me, but the longer this goes on, the more I find myself agreeing."

The girl provided a good area to explore and Zax jumped on it. "Twenty credits for a great observation. It's true that being members of the Crew requires us to serve and protect the civilians. They obviously benefit from this a great deal, but what do we get out of the bargain?"

"I can't think of anything we get from the civilians, sir. They get all the benefit and we bear all the cost."

Zax smiled at her. A year ago he would have had the exact same viewpoint, and it would have stemmed from the same place of ignorance. These cadets had never experienced a single direct interaction with a civilian. Their fellow humans, who actually outnumbered the cadets one hundred to one among the Ship's inhabitants who were not in cryostorage, were nearly as foreign and unknown as the aliens they were training to battle.

The civilians ceased being an abstract concept for Zax once he was dropped from Flight Ops and landed at the bottom of the Crew hierarchy. Waste Systems managed the Ship's sewage and because it involved the most disgusting tasks it was staffed almost exclusively by civilians. Zax didn't interact with them all of the time, but as the most junior member of the Crew on the small operations team, it was usually his job to assist whenever they needed help. He had been surprised to learn the civilians almost universally felt antagonism towards the Crew, though he hadn't yet been able to prod any of them into sharing enough to help him understand their antipathy. Regardless, he had come to develop some small measure of appreciation for the work they performed.

"I'm assigned to a part of the Ship where I interact with civilians all of the time—excuse me, would you like to share what's so funny?"

The cadet who made the "idiot" comment earlier had leaned over and whispered something to the girl sitting next to him. The friend started giggling and Zax decided to call them out rather than allow them to run roughshod over his lesson.

The boy stared defiantly at Zax. "You were talking about where you work, and I observed how we are all well aware because we can generally smell the stink on you."

The words stung, especially because Zax knew they were true. He fought to keep the shame hidden as he refused to give the cadet the satisfaction of seeing even a hint of his self-loathing. Slamming the boy with a massive slug of demerits would be delightful, but Zax knew doing so could potentially backfire if the cadet appealed. A key feature of the Leaderboard system was that all officers and instructors knew they would be personally docked ten times the number of any demerits if they were shown to have assessed them out of self-interest or spite. Though they were clearly intended to offend, there was technically nothing inaccurate about the Gamma's words and he had delivered them with a neutral tone. If the boy appealed any excessive demerits he would certainly prevail, so Zax focused only on what was incontrovertible.

"Twenty demerits for each of you for the interruption."

The boy grinned once again as he clearly seemed to believe having fun at Zax's expense was worth the cost. Zax swallowed his aggravation and continued.

"As I was saying, I've had a chance to work with civilians extensively in the past year. What I've learned in that time is they do serve an important role on board. Operating and maintaining this Ship requires a host of tasks that anyone in the Crew would hate. These jobs don't require much in the way of skill, but the Ship wouldn't survive without them.

"Maintaining the civilian population does require effort and resources, but throughout history they have typically caused far fewer headaches than they are right now. We don't have to provide them with much beyond protection and food rations, so the benefits they provide usually outweigh their costs. As you get older and have exposure to more of the day-to-day life on board, you'll come to appreciate their role more."

The girl in the front row raised her hand again, and Zax gestured for her to speak.

"It reminds me of a quote from one of Earth's great philosophers. *'From each according to his ability, to each according to his contribution.'*"

Zax grinned. "Great way to tie it all together. Fifty credits. Now, let's put aside the civilians for a while and dive into how the Ship generates artificial gravity."

CHAPTER FOUR

Ouch!

Zax finished with the Gammas and headed to his advanced Plug training. He had become quite adept over the past year at using his implant for communication as well as virtual activities like his flight simulator, but it was finally time for him to learn about interacting more directly with the Ship and its various components. He entered the training compartment and found a tiny vehicle positioned at the entrance of a maze. The maze led into an opaque box which was about half again the size of the maze. The instructor stood as Zax entered the room.

"Good morning, cadet. We're here to complete the final stage of your Plug training. If you successfully complete this task, then you'll be granted full access to all of your implant functionality. Are you ready?"

Zax nodded and the instructor continued. "The past year has allowed your Plug to completely meld with the neural pathways within your brain. While you've accomplished a lot with it in this time, you've only scratched the surface of the capabilities the Plug can ultimately provide. You'll now learn how to connect directly with the Ship's physical systems via your thoughts."

The instructor turned and pointed at the vehicle and maze. "Your task is to maneuver that vehicle through the maze using only your mind. The path through the visible portion of the maze leads into the black box. The box covers the final portion of the maze, which you'll need to navigate by relying on the sensory information being sent from the vehicle rather than what comes from your own body. Go."

The instructor sat down. Zax looked at him expecting more information, but the man only returned his gaze impassively. After a few secs it became clear he had said all he intended to say. Zax needed to figure it out on his own.

He glanced around the room to see if anything else was supposed to play a role in the exercise and saw nothing. Zax looked at the vehicle again as he thought about controlling it and was surprised to notice a slight aura around it. The aura brightened as Zax focused more intensely on it, and then a prompt appeared in his vision.

Access vehicle controls, yes/no?

Of course the answer was yes, but Zax wasn't entirely sure how to select his choice. He stared at the word 'Yes' floating in his vision, but there was no aura around it. After a few mins, he became frustrated and thought about how he wanted to give up and forget about the vehicle. At that very same instant, the text prompt disappeared from sight.

That was interesting. It was almost like Zax's decision to give up on the vehicle made the prompt go away. But hadn't he thought about controlling the vehicle earlier and nothing happened?

Zax stared intently at the vehicle and once again the text prompt appeared asking whether he wanted to access it. This time, he did not think about selecting 'Yes' as much as he thought about controlling the vehicle. He heard a *click* and its electric motor switched on and spun up with a *whirrrr*. At the same time, the text prompt disappeared and was replaced with a series of icons. There were arrows which suggested movement in different directions, plus and minus signs which hinted at the ability to speed up/slow down, and a few other icons which were initially incomprehensible.

The instructor finally spoke. "Can you explain what just happened there, cadet?"

"I think so, sir. When the prompt first appeared in my vision, I was focused on choosing 'Yes' in order to access the vehicle's controls. I got frustrated because nothing happened regardless of what I tried.

Eventually, I realized I wasn't supposed to literally choose 'Yes' or 'No', but instead needed to focus on the action and outcome I wanted as a result of that choice. If I wanted to control the vehicle, then it would be under my command. If I wanted to give up on the vehicle, then I would no longer control it."

"Well done, cadet. That's the critical realization which proves hard for many people who are relatively new to their implants to grasp. Whenever you look at items on board the Ship and think about interacting with them, you will see prompts and other information in your vision which are intended to help you understand what kind of commands are available. For example, right now you are seeing icons which show what is possible for you to do with the vehicle under your control. These are just *hints* to help you shape your intention, not actual controls for you to interact with. As soon as you decide your intention is to move the vehicle forward in the maze, it will move forward until you intend for it to stop. Easier said than done, of course, but once you're able to make that first leap, you stand a very good chance of quickly mastering the rest."

Zax had been getting frustrated at the lack of vehicle movement as he stared at the forward arrow, but the last portion of the instructor's guidance finally registered. *Intention* is the key. Don't focus on what you see in your vision, focus on what you intend to happen. He took a deep breath and thought about how he wanted the vehicle to move forward. The wheels spun ever so slightly, and it began a slow roll away from Zax into the maze.

"Awesome!" Zax exclaimed.

"There you go, cadet. Let's see you make it all the way through, though, before we start getting too excited."

Zax smiled at the gentle admonition and turned back to the maze. He identified the path to the black box and focused on keeping the vehicle heading in the right direction. It was moving smoothly through the middle of an S curve when the vehicle crashed for the first time. Zax was certain he wanted the vehicle to turn left, but it had turned right instead and lodged against the wall. He reversed to set up another attempt, but once again the vehicle turned the wrong way at the most critical time.

This pattern repeated a few times until the solution finally dawned on Zax. He turned the vehicle smoothly when it moved away from him because the direction of the turn as he perceived it was the same direction as it applied to the vehicle. His left and the vehicle's left matched. When the vehicle headed towards him, however, there was a difference between what he saw as being a left turn and what the vehicle would see as a left turn. Zax's left would be right for the vehicle and vice versa. With this in mind, he focused on directions from the vehicle's perspective rather than his own and successfully navigated the remaining turns.

The vehicle reached the final straightaway which led into the black box, and Zax pushed it to go faster. The vehicle zoomed ahead and disappeared into the box only to come to a crashing halt a moment later. Zax looked over at the instructor, but he no longer watched Zax's progress and instead stared at his slate.

Zax reevaluated the information icons within his field of vision and one caught his attention. It was an eyeball, which seemed to suggest there might be a way for Zax to see things from the vehicle's perspective. He thought about what it would be like to look out the windshield of the vehicle, but nothing happened. That wasn't entirely accurate. There was a slight shimmer in his vision and Zax experienced the strangest sensation in his body. It reminded him of the feeling he got sometimes when he desperately needed to sneeze but couldn't. Zax closed his eyes and tried again.

WHOOSH! The sensation was like nothing Zax had ever experienced and he involuntarily exclaimed, "Whoa!" It felt like he zoomed down a tunnel at near lightspeed only to find himself looking through the vehicle's front window at the end of it. Zax wondered if his outburst caught the instructor's attention but didn't want to open his eyes and risk losing the view from the vehicle's perspective. It had run up against a wall so Zax backed it up and adjusted course.

Left turn—right turn—dead end—back up—try again.

Dead end—try again.

Dead end—try again.

The maze was more challenging without the overhead view he enjoyed before the vehicle entered the box, but Zax didn't mind the fits and starts. They provided opportunities to adapt his mind to working from a new and entirely crazy vantage point. His body was outside the maze, but the Plug did an amazing job of forcing his brain to think he was piloting the tiny vehicle from the inside.

Zax guessed he was nearing the end of the maze when the vehicle entered a long straightaway similar to the one it had traversed immediately before entering the box. He paused the vehicle for a moment when he noticed something different about the maze's floor directly ahead of it. The floor in earlier portions of the maze was the same color as the walls and ceiling, but in the stretch ahead it glowed a bright red. Zax was convinced he was heading the correct way so he moved forward, albeit slowly.

The vehicle's tires crossed into the red portion of the floor, and Zax immediately noticed his feet getting warmer. The heat reached a painful intensity a sec later and his eyes shot open in a panic.

"Ouch!"

Zax looked down to investigate. The pain had disappeared immediately along with his view out the front of the vehicle's window. His feet appeared perfectly normal. Zax glanced over and saw the instructor smiling.

"Don't worry—everyone reacts the same way which is what makes this my favorite part of the session. There are a couple of key lessons you need to take away from this section of the maze, cadet. First, you clearly noticed the floor immediately before the exit is heated. The purpose of this is to illustrate how sensory information you experience via your Plug is not limited to visuals. If you are connected to something which can transmit sound, then you will hear sound. Here, the vehicle was configured to transmit the temperature encountered by its wheels, and you experienced heat on your feet. It was not true physical pain, of course, but the Plug convinced your brain otherwise. With practice, you'll learn to tolerate this 'phantom pain' in order to use it for informational purposes without suffering the emotional response you just experienced."

The instructor grinned even more broadly and continued. "The other thing to understand is how the sensory data you experienced went away the instant you opened your eyes. This is to be expected at your age and with your level of Plug experience. The most challenging part of using your implant is forcing your body's sensory information into the background so you can focus on whatever input is coming from your Plug. This ability is greatly enhanced by removing visual stimulation, which is why you often see even advanced folks close their eyes if they are trying to do something particularly difficult via their Plug."

The instructor looked back down at his slate. "Your elapsed time for a first trip through the maze was better than average, but you need to make it through a lot faster before I can sign off and say you're fully cleared to use your Plug. Let's get the vehicle set up at the beginning again."

CHAPTER FIVE

You eat it.

Zax left the Plug training with a bounce in his step having been given final clearance to use his Plug to fully interact with the Ship's systems. His excitement quickly faded, however, once he thought about the day's next destination. Zax's work in Waste Systems might become slightly more interesting now that he could take full advantage of his Plug's capabilities, but he didn't hold out much hope. Final Plug activation was a nice milestone, but Zax regretfully concluded it was most likely meaningless given his current career status.

He had even more time to ponder how much he hated his job when the trip to Waste Systems took longer than expected. Tube service between the start and end points of his journey was available but was routed in a way that added 5 mins to his trip. The Crew who managed the Tube had become quite adept at modifying routings quickly in response to the civilian disruptions. It only took one instance of an Omega being killed when she unknowingly emerged from a Tube junction into the middle of rampaging civilians that riot avoidance become a critical mission for the service's operators.

Zax tried to push aside his frustrations as he arrived on station. He was grateful for the boring hours at work which provided time to pursue other interests, but nonetheless felt the typical pangs of regret when he thought back to the thrills of his prior job in Flight Ops. Compared to that nerve center with one massive panorama that looked into space and another that commanded a view of the bustling flight deck, the windowless confines of the Waste Systems operations center provided all the excitement of a maintenance closet. There were only two other Crew assigned to the department, and he spoke to the first as he sat down at his terminal.

"Good morning, ma'am. Anything special you need me to do today?"

Lieutenant Salmea was Zax's direct supervisor. He had concluded that she must have arrived at the bottom of the heap thanks to chronic indifference. She once again lived up (down?) to this assessment by keeping her dull gray eyes fixed on her slate as she remained slumped in her seat and barely managed a shrug in response.

Zax next turned to check whether the hatch to Westerick's office was open. Major Westerick held the title of department chief. Zax hadn't experienced enough direct interactions with the man to ascertain whether it was too much incompetence or too little intelligence which had saddled him with such a hideous assignment. The days when Westerick had ventured out of his office in the year since Zax had arrived could be counted on one hand.

Before Zax could dive into more work on his flight simulator, he paused to greet Imair as she entered the compartment. A civilian who was somewhere in her late forties, Imair wore her mousy brown hair in a short bob that was as indistinctly efficient as the manner in which she did her job. Her small stature and quiet demeanor allowed her to fade into the background. It was only Zax's careful observations of the civilian workers' behavior patterns that revealed her position atop their unofficial hierarchy. If she was bothered by having to show deference to a Crew member a third her age, she kept it hidden as she addressed him.

"Good morning, sir. I'm sorry to interrupt your work, but we're stuck with something and hoped you might be able to provide some guidance."

"Sure thing, Imair. Lead the way."

Zax stood and followed the civilian out of the clean and well-lit operations compartment and then down the series of ladders which provided access to the Waste Systems work areas. As they descended deeper, the surroundings became progressively more dim and filthy. He had eventually become acclimated to the nasal reminders of what Waste Systems dealt with, but the omnipresent scent of human waste in the lower levels could still trigger Zax's gag reflex once in a while. His trips into the work areas always provided a stark reminder of just how far his career had fallen.

Imair was about to lead Zax through a hatch into the maintenance hub when a young, high-pitched voice called out with a level of cheery enthusiasm that belied the grim environment.

"Hello, sir!"

Nolly bolted down the passageway towards them. The eight-year-old civilian was practically swimming in a mismatched uniform riddled with rips and smeared with filth. The boy skidded to a halt and brushed his shaggy blonde hair out of his eyes as he looked up at Zax with a big grin.

"Hey, Nolly. I've got a surprise for you."

Zax reached into his pocket and pulled out the apple he had taken from the mess hall. He held it out to the boy who appraised it with a confused look.

"What is it, sir?"

Zax was momentarily taken aback. It had been surprising enough when the boy had shared a few days earlier how he had never eaten a piece of fruit, but to learn he didn't even recognize an apple when held in front of him was positively shocking.

"Umm, it's an apple—a piece of fruit. You eat it. Take a bite."

The boy took the apple and gave it a small, tentative nibble. Nolly's expression transformed from apprehension to pure joy. Two huge bites followed in quick succession after which he used the heel of his palm to wipe the resultant chin drippings back into his mouth.

Zax smiled at the boy's exuberance and swiveled to Imair, curious as to whether she shared his appreciation. She wasn't looking at Nolly but instead had fixed her gaze on Zax with what appeared to be bewilderment. As Zax turned to her, Imair's expression switched almost instantly back to neutral and she addressed the young civilian.

"Put that in your pocket, Nolly, and go find someplace where you can finish it without anyone seeing you. When you get into the middle, there are going to be tough, stringy pieces and hard, black things called seeds. You can eat those bits if you choose, but they won't taste nearly as good as the outer portion."

The boy bolted, but before disappearing around the corner he looked back over his shoulder and shouted. "Thank you, sir!"

Imair turned and walked through the hatch. Zax followed being sure to scan his eyes all around as he entered the compartment. Mikedo's lesson during his Marine training about gaining immediate awareness of new surroundings had stuck with Zax. A group of civilians huddled around a display. They looked up as Imair approached, and the lone male in the group spoke.

"We've continued to troubleshoot, but we just can't figure out where the fault is coming from."

Imair turned back to Zax. "Sir, the system keeps reporting a fault we can't resolve. We've even tried resetting the whole module, but nothing has worked. We're hoping you might have some ideas."

"I bet you've focused on the subsystems in compartment 50-H in trying to sort this out," Zax offered after a quick look at the display. "This circuit is unique because it has a special offshoot which leads into 51-F as well. Let's go take a look there."

Zax exited the compartment and Imair spoke as she caught up. "Must be nice to just use your Plug to access the schematics and get an answer so quickly. We've had a team of five racking our brains for eighty-nine mins, and you just walk in and solve it after seventeen secs."

"I actually didn't use my Plug," Zax replied. "I studied all of the Waste Systems schematics when I first started here. That circuit stood out as an oddball since it was the only one that splits the way it does. I figured one day it would cause an issue like this, and it looks like I was right."

For the second time in a few mins, Zax felt like he had perplexed Imair based on her facial expression. "You mean, you've committed the entire system to memory?"

"I don't know about the whole system," Zax grinned, "but hopefully I've managed to remember the most interesting bits."

Zax halted at a small access port, but Imair kept walking without noticing. She quickly realized, stopped, and looked back at him.

"Sir, we need to keep going this way to get to 51-F."

"Yes, that's the best route if we want to stick to the main passageways and ladders. The fastest route, though, is to use the maintenance network. There's a laddered shaft that will let us get up to 51 and the tunnels between here and there are almost entirely walkable. There is one four meter stretch where we'll have to crawl, but even factoring that in this should still save us 156 secs of travel time." Zax smiled. "Well—it will save us that travel time as long as you trust me and don't stop to question every turn we take."

Imair stared at him impassively for a moment before she spoke. "My apologies, sir. Let me guess— you've memorized the routing of all the maintenance tunnels too."

"At least the interesting ones." Zax replied as he opened the port.

CHAPTER SIX

Why the apple?

Imair dutifully followed Zax in silence as he led her through a series of tunnels and eventually back through the main passageway until they reached compartment 51-F. She watched over his shoulder as he removed an access panel and got to work.

The relay which Zax suspected was misfiring displayed the same aura the small vehicle had during his Plug training. He focused on the device and was excited to be presented with a series of options including one that allowed him to see the inside of it as if it was transparent. After a few mins of poking around he announced his findings.

"Well—this time I did actually use my Plug and confirmed we've got a misfiring relay here. I think I've got it successfully recalibrated, so let's have your team reset the system and see what happens."

Imair walked across the room, lifted a communicator off the bulkhead, and passed along Zax's instructions. She put the communicator back down after a moment of listening to the response.

"I'm sorry, sir, but the reset cycle on that circuit takes 321 secs. Would you mind waiting with me to see whether it's really fixed?"

"Not a problem. I've got a short piece of reading to do, so I'm going to focus on my Plug while we wait."

Zax had been reading for 148 secs when Imair's voice drew his attention. He was so taken aback by a civilian having the temerity to interrupt him that he didn't initially comprehend what she said and was forced to ask that she repeat herself.

"Why the apple?"

He was momentarily stumped but deciphered she must be asking about his gift to Nolly. "Why not?"

"I'm sorry, sir, we just don't typically experience acts of kindness from members of the Crew. Most of you treat us like interchangeable cogs. In fact, I would be shocked if Lieutenant Salmea even knows my name."

Zax thought for a few moments before replying. "We had been talking a few days earlier, and Nolly mentioned he had never eaten a piece of fruit. I was reminded of it when I walked by a pile of apples in the Crew mess earlier, so I grabbed one for him to try."

Imair stared at him for a few uncomfortably long beats before she answered. "All the same, sir, I would respectfully request that you not do anything like that again. He's so young and I don't want him to get any wrong ideas—about food availability or about what kind of behavior he should expect from Crew he interacts with."

"What's the big deal about one apple, Imair?"

"Sir, do you know how long it's been since there has been *any* fruit available in the civilian mess? I wasn't that much older than you are now the last time I ate an apple."

Zax was stumped for a reply. Imair had no reason to concoct a story like this, but her words made no sense. He couldn't begin to count the number of times he had thrown away some random piece of fruit he had decided he didn't actually want after taking one bite. How could there not be enough fruit to go around if there was enough for the Crew to waste? He was trying to figure out a coherent response when Imair laughed and spoke again.

"Look at your gears grinding, sir. It appears you may have a misfiring relay of your own. You folks in the Crew really don't have the slightest clue what our lives are like, do you, sir?"

"How could we, Imair?" Zax was exasperated and felt no compunction to hide it. "Most of us don't ever get a chance to interact with civilians directly. I've been able to over the past year only because I've been stuck working here, but even then I can't get anyone to actually talk with me about anything. It's clear you civilians don't like the Crew very much, but no one will give me the slightest hint as to why. Any questions I ask generally end the conversation."

Imair stared at him thoughtfully for a while before finally speaking. "Honestly addressing questions about sensitive topics is a great way for a civilian to find herself on the short list to being Culled, sir. The fact you can't comprehend that is just further evidence of how huge the divide really is. You seem like you're genuinely interested, though, and I hope we have an opportunity at some point soon for you to gain the understanding you seek."

The communicator buzzed and Imair strode back to where it was mounted on the bulkhead. She answered and then listened for a few moments before thanking the person on the other end and placing the communicator back down. "I'm sorry, sir, but the fault is still present after the reset."

Zax wanted to forget about the relay and keep talking about the fruit and other areas of civilian life, but Imair's tone of voice had shifted back to pure business. He filed away their conversation for further investigation later and closed his eyes to check something via his Plug. "I guess we'll just have to replace that relay altogether, but I can't find a new one in stock anywhere nearby. Let me reach out to Major Westerick and see if he knows where to find one."

Zax turned away from Imair to focus on his Plug, and after a moment the Major responded to Zax's ping.

"What?"

"I'm sorry to bother you, sir, but I'm in compartment 51-F and we have diagnosed a faulty relay. I've checked the stocks, and I can't find a replacement for it anywhere. Do you have any suggestions for where I might be able to track down another one?"

"Wait." After a few moments of silence the Major continued. *"I've accessed the inventory records and found one in a different section. I've sent you the location and a one-time pass for security."*

Westerick cut their connection. No pleasantries, no small talk, no chit chat. It was the first time Zax had bothered the Major in months, and yet the conversation over their Plugs was markedly less pleasant and cheerful than speaking with a Replicator.

Zax checked the location of the storage locker which Westerick had identified and raised an eyebrow at the realization it was deep in Engineering—a region of the Ship that was adjacent to Waste Systems yet might as well be worlds away. He had studied its schematics in his spare time and knew Engineering was a warren of compartments, some small, some massive, but he had never actually seen any of them firsthand since access was forbidden without the proper security clearance. Clearance he now possessed—at least for this single visit. He grinned at the thought of a trip away from Waste Systems as he turned to face Imair.

"The Major located a replacement for me, but it's in a high security area of the Ship where civilians aren't allowed. Should I meet you back here when I return?"

"I'm actually off duty in a few mins, sir. We can deal with this later. Thank you."

She turned and walked out of the compartment. Zax worried for a moment about the pregnant pause before she had replied. He figured it must still be about the stupid apple so he pushed the thought aside as he walked to the nearest Tube junction and made his way to Engineering.

CHAPTER SEVEN

Hello, Zax.

The Tube came to a stop and Zax exited into the very non-welcoming gaze of six fully armed Marines. Well, it was actually more like the gaze of one Marine since the other five were engrossed in an argument among themselves and paid him zero attention.

"Well, well, well. Look who we have here."

The voice and its sarcastic tone triggered recognition before Zax's brain could fully recover from the shock of encountering the stern Marine with his pale skin and close-cropped white hair. Zax hadn't seen Sergeant Bailee since the man told him about the outcome of the final training evaluation for him and Kalare—the eval which cleared Zax for the fateful planetary expedition with the Marines. It seemed like the man still nursed a grudge about Zax bumping into him and spilling his coffee during their first encounter, so Zax was on guard for the beating he was sure would eventually come.

"Huh...hello, Sergeant Bailee. I've been cleared by Major Westerick in Waste Systems to access a storage locker in Engineering and retrieve a spare part."

The Marine closed his eyes for a moment and nodded as he validated Zax's security clearance via his Plug. "I see that. Well, I guess you're in for a special surprise then."

Zax fretted about what the icy glimmer in the Marine's eyes meant as he followed him through the hatch into Engineering Control. The shock of encountering Sergeant Bailee was exceeded ten-fold when Zax discovered Aleron standing across the compartment and gawping at him. Encountering the cadet who had bullied him interminably was certainly unexpected in this particular compartment, but Zax wasn't convinced that would be anything Bailee would qualify as a "special surprise."

"Hello, Zax."

It had been a year since he last heard it, but Zax recognized when his name was being voiced through teeth clenched around an unlit cigar. His blood went cold. He hadn't reconnoitered the compartment as he entered and had missed the Flight Boss standing just inside the hatch. The Omega leaned casually against the bulkhead, slate in hand, square head covered as always by his backwards-facing workcap.

"Ummm...huh...huh...hello, s-s-s-sir."

Zax's legs had turned to jelly. It took every ounce of willpower to prevent himself from collapsing to the floor. Another familiar voice called out.

"Zax! What are the chances of seeing you here!"

Kalare bounded across the compartment. She grabbed Zax by the arm and addressed the Boss.

"Sir—may I please borrow Zax for a few mins?"

The Flight Boss went back to looking at his slate by way of silent dismissal, and Kalare dragged Zax to an area devoid of workstations at the far side of the compartment. So many overwhelming emotions flooded Zax that his mind might have shut down and attempted to float away out of self-preservation if it wasn't for the anchoring grasp of Kalare's hand clenched around his arm.

As Zax attempted to collect his wits, Aleron watched the whole drama unfold from across the compartment with his mouth twisted into a spiteful grin. It finally registered that his long-time tormentor was wearing a red Engineering uniform, and Zax recalled hearing about the boy's recent reassignment into this section.

"Zax! You've got to get it together!" Kalare was close enough that the spittle punctuating her vehement whispers stung his face. "It's crazy obvious how you're barely keeping your head straight right now—snap out of it!"

Zax took a few deep breaths. The entire compartment gradually came into sharp focus as he established situational awareness. Numerous Crew were present and appeared to be hard at work, but a few faces stood out. The Chief Engineer was recognizable from her many appearances on newsvids. She finished conversing with a subordinate and walked towards the Flight Boss. Aleron had turned back to his work, but every few moments would look back over his shoulder to check in on what was going on. Bailee stood by the hatch and observed Zax and Kalare with a stony expression.

Zax took one final deep breath. "Thanks, Kalare. I clearly wasn't prepared to run into this particular mix of people."

Kalare smiled. "I know. It's definitely your all-time favorite Crew! What are you doing here?"

"I've got to pick up a spare part from an equipment locker in the next compartment." Zax grimaced. "Of course, it's through the hatch next to Aleron's workstation."

Kalare appraised Aleron and her smile widened a little further. "Don't worry about him, Zax. That one is definitely not worth getting worked up about."

"Easy for you to say. Let me go find what I need before I forget the whole reason why I'm here. Then maybe we can chat for a min on my way back out."

Zax was torn between quizzing Kalare on what she was doing in Engineering and getting as far away from the Boss and Sergeant Bailee as fast as he could.

Escape ultimately proved most attractive and Zax hustled towards the next compartment to find the equipment locker. He was so intent on completing his errand that he missed Aleron's leg shooting into his path and went sprawling into a stack of equipment piled next to the hatch. The clanging racket drew the attention of everyone in the compartment, and the Boss and Chief Engineer laughed out loud at his pratfall.

Humiliation wafted off Zax as thick as the stench of excrement back in Waste Systems. What made it even more unbearable was how Aleron immediately turned and extended a hand to assist him up off the deck. Having successfully doled out his abuse in plain sight, the bully was now trying to look pleasant and helpful in front of the officers.

Zax wanted to slug Aleron but knew immediate retribution would earn him nothing but a heap of demerits with the Boss present to be witness and dole out punishment. He forced himself to instead be satisfied with slapping away the boy's outstretched hand. Zax rose and was dusting himself off while everyone gawked at him when the hatch from the main passageway opened. Something odd about the Marine guard's expression as he entered caught Zax's attention.

The unmistakable *crack* of a blaster echoed within the compartment. The Marine's bewildered countenance shifted to one of intense pain as his stomach blossomed into the gory, red mess of an exit wound. Before he could even consider how to react, a haze of light blue gas filled the space and Zax felt his consciousness wane as he slumped back to the deck. His last thoughts were dominated by utter confusion. How the hell could the compartment's entryway possibly be filled with a group of civilians who carried blasters and wore supplemental breathers?

CHAPTER EIGHT

Pretty effective, if I do say so myself.

A slap to his face dragged Zax back to Engineering Control. He was initially overwhelmed by a coppery smell so thick he assumed his nose was bleeding. He opened his eyes and discovered it emanated instead from five dead Marines piled an arm's length away and surrounded by a pool of congealing blood. Only Sergeant Bailee remained alive from the six who had guarded the entrance to the compartment. The sergeant was bound with his hands behind his back in the same fashion as Zax. The Marine also wore the same type of black device around his neck which Zax could feel had been fastened around his own.

Zax looked around and realized all the other Crew who had been present before the intrusion remained alive and now sat on the deck with their hands bound and identical black devices around their necks. A dozen civilians were arrayed around the compartment with blasters pointed at the Crew and fingers poised on triggers. The only civilian who wasn't armed with a blaster carried himself like he was the leader and stood off to the side focused on a device in his hand. He was shorter and far skinnier than the rest, with long, greasy black hair that covered his eyes and fell almost to his shoulders.

In addition to the civilians with their weapons, Zax noticed a couple dozen crates had also appeared while he was unconscious. They bore no external markings but seemed to have been intentionally arranged around the compartment.

The giant, brawny civilian whose slap had stirred Zax moved on to deliver the same rude awakening first to Aleron and then to another red-shirted Engineering cadet who were both seated to his left. The last cadet required three slaps before he was finally conscious, each one progressively more harsh. Once the boy finally stirred, the civilian remained next to him and then looked up and nodded his blocky, bald head towards the short man with the device.

The leader brushed his oily bangs out of his eyes, cleared his throat, and spoke as he moved towards the engineering cadet.

"Greetings *fine* Crew members. It is a *distinct pleasure* to make your acquaintance. We're going to be spending quite a bit of time together, so I'll introduce myself. My name is Rege, and my friends and I have come here for a special visit with the Chief Engineer. You can imagine our great delight to learn that, completely by chance, we'll get to chat with the Flight Boss as well!

"As *brilliant* as all of you Crew are, you've no doubt noticed how each of you has been fitted with a black collar. Don't try to remove yours because I guarantee you won't like what happens if it's tampered with. The collars are fun devices we've been working on for the past few months and had a chance to test out on a few of your fellow Crew who we kidnapped during recent riots. Your collar serves two purposes. First, it disrupts your Plug in such a way as to render it temporarily useless. We'll shortly have control of all communication channels anyways, but we also wanted to be sure you couldn't interact with anything around you. Second, it guarantees your complete and undivided attention and cooperation. By way of demonstration, please watch the cadet sitting next to my colleague here."

Rege gestured at the cadet who was sitting to the left of Aleron—the one who had required three slaps to awaken. When he realized the man was talking about him, the cadet's eyes went wide with fear. A moment later he appeared to be gripped by excruciating pain as blood streamed out of both nostrils, his face contorted, and his body flailed. He continued to writhe violently for at least ten secs until his head collapsed to his chest and his body went still.

Zax observed the reactions of the others in the silence that followed. Kalare sat with her eyes twisted shut. Aleron looked terrified and was likely thinking it could just as easily have been him sitting there dead. The Chief Engineer appeared to waver between fury and despair. Sergeant Bailee was doing everything he could to kill Rege with nothing available to him but his glare. Only the Flight Boss seemed unmoved. He must have dropped his cigar when he was knocked out by the gas and now sat, mouth empty, stoically staring straight ahead but focused on nothing.

After letting everyone marinate in the cadet's death for a min, Rege continued.

"Pretty effective, if I do say so myself. The bad news is they have a short range, so that's why we'll have to keep most of you bound and jammed in together. The good news is we can choose to hit you with something less than the full blast which I just gave the cadet. Get out of hand a little and we can give you a quick jolt as a reminder about the penalty for non-compliance. Get out of hand a lot and—well— there's room on the heap for more."

Rege laughed as the bald civilian casually tossed the cadet's lifeless body onto the pile of dead Marines. He then looked down at his device before speaking again.

"Everyone sit tight. You're going to get a full explanation about what is happening. In 3—2—1—"

Klaxons wailed and the lights switched to the pulsing amber which indicated the Captain had changed the Ship to Condition 1. Her face appeared on all of the vidscreens around the compartment.

"This message is being broadcast to everyone on board the Ship—Crew and civilians alike. We are now at our highest alert level, Condition 1. This is not because of an external attack by aliens but rather due to an internal attack by a small number of disaffected civilians. Today's actions are slightly larger and more coordinated than the recent isolated riots, but they will be put down just as quickly and just as easily.

"The civilian disruptions of the past year have led us to redeploy our Marines so we could be thoroughly prepared for the potential of a wider attack like this one. They have been relocated from their centralized barracks and are now widely dispersed in garrisons throughout the Ship. Fifty thousand Marines in full battle gear are coming on station within the next ninety secs. For my fellow Crew who may be in danger from this civilian disruption—hold tight. The cavalry is on the way. Keep your heads down and before you know it, all of the hostile civilians in your vicinity will be neutralized."

As the Captain spoke, her image was replaced by video footage of Marines engaged in combat with various aliens. As scary as some of the aliens looked, they paled in comparison to the fearsome appearance of the Marines wearing their combat load. Zax shuddered at the thought of what a pissed off Marine in full battle gear would do once unleashed among a population of civilians. The invisibility offered by their ChamWare would provide freedom of movement throughout the Ship, and their combat armor would easily protect them from the lightweight weapons the civilians possessed. The group who took Engineering hostage overwhelmed five Marines who wore no armor and, frankly, weren't paying much attention, but they'd be dead within moments of encountering even a single alert Marine in full gear. Zax remained worried about what might happen in the meantime but was relieved to know they would be rescued soon.

Zax gauged the civilians' reaction to the news of their impending demise. He was shocked to see Rege and a couple others laughing among themselves while they watched the combat footage. He would thoroughly enjoy watching the man die a gruesome death after witnessing how the Engineering cadet had suffered.

The Captain reappeared and started to speak, but her voice cut out even though her lips continued to move. She soon realized her audio wasn't being broadcast and turned to someone of view. Her image on the vidscreen became wavy and then pixelated before it disappeared and she was replaced by a picture Zax instantly recognized—the cockpit of the human spacecraft he and Mikedo had discovered. It was a screencap which must have been taken from the video Zax had broadcast in Flight Ops back when he confronted the Flight Boss. The human writing and image of Earth were clearly visible. A voice spoke over the image.

"Greetings, fellow humans."

CHAPTER NINE

We know they are out there somewhere.

"**G**reetings, fellow humans. I repeat myself because I must emphasize my words are not intended solely for the civilians listening. This is an urgent message which is critical for all of us on the Ship to hear and understand—not only the ten million civilians but also the one hundred thousand Crew who can hear my voice.

"The image on the screen before you is one which few of you have seen even though many of you have heard rumors about its existence. Today I'm going to share with you its full truth. A truth which will explain why a group of us were compelled to take drastic action over the past year.

"We all learn from an early age the history of our Ship. Earth was near death and sent forth this vessel as its only lifeboat to protect the remnants of humanity. Our Mission was to save our species by seeding the universe with colonies populated by the billion people waiting to be revived from our cryosleep holds. The scientists who sent us into space believed we would spend a hundred years exploring nearby galaxies and eventually find enough new homes that humankind would be guaranteed survival.

"Unfortunately, the universe is a barren and nearly lifeless place. Even though Earth's astronomers believed there would be millions of Earth-equivalent worlds spread among the stars, we've since discovered the planetary conditions necessary to support human life are rare. Even worse, those isolated rocks where we might be able to eke out even a pathetic existence are frequently inhabited by violent aliens who seek similar conditions and will fight tooth and claw to keep what they've got for themselves.

"We are now five thousand years into our one hundred year Mission. Throughout the generations, our situation has grown more and more challenging. In recent years, many of us have concluded the Ship is tipping over into the same death spiral which befell Earth. Too many people barely survive by slaving away their entire lives for the benefit of too few, while our meager remaining resources are hoarded by the powerful at the expense of the weak. Look around and it's obvious to even the youngest child the

Ship will not last another five thousand years. We'll be lucky if it manages to last another hundred. Of course, its ultimate disintegration will impact Crew and civilian alike."

Something nagged at Zax after a few mins of listening. The voice had been modulated to disguise the speaker, but there was something about the speech pattern that seemed familiar. As for the content of the message, Zax had no idea where this talk of slavery was coming from and who exactly might be hoarding what resources, but he agreed with the person's assessment of the Ship. As long as he had been alive, it had been clear the pace of decay among the Ship's critical systems was accelerating towards a point where all of their maintenance efforts would no longer keep ahead of the damage. Hell, it was amazing the FTL drive had lasted so long. It was the most critical system on board which also had no redundancy. It might not occur in his lifetime, but Zax was certain the Ship was sliding inexorably towards an irreparable state. The voice continued.

"Even though all of us who have given this any significant thought have recognized the Ship's condition will ultimately prove fatal and our Mission will fail, we never saw a better alternative than to press ahead and seek out the next new world in the next new system. What else could we do? Earth was behind us somewhere, but what would be the sense in going back to a dead planet. We've left plenty of colonies in our wake, but not a single one of those

planets was sufficient to support the ten million of us who are awake, much less the billion who still wait in cryosleep. If there's nothing behind us but death or misery, then why not press forward and hope for the best.

"This equation changed one year ago, though the Crew's leadership has done their utmost to keep this fact hidden. A group of Marines discovered irrefutable evidence the Ship is not the only representative of humanity traveling the stars. The image on the screen was taken during a planetary expedition and shows the wreckage of a fighter craft which is not associated with the Ship and yet is clearly human in origin. Look at the writing in the cockpit! Look at that picture of Earth! Even though the Omega puppets who lead the Crew and the Ship's Artifical Intelligence which pulls their strings tried to suppress and discredit this evidence, I'm here today as emphatic proof it was impossible for them to do so. We are not alone! There are more humans traveling the stars—humans who have the means and ability to explore distant planets!"

Zax didn't need to be told the image of the human fighter was legitimate since he had seen the craft firsthand. He had never admitted this fact to anyone other than Kalare in an effort to protect himself but instead concocted a story where he was only passing along what Mikedo had sent him in her final message. When Zax first revealed the video, the Omegas who ran the Ship tried to bully the few people who saw it into forgetting about it altogether. When that strategy failed and news of the video became too widespread to ignore, they pursued a different approach. Alpha, the root node of the Ship's AI, produced "evidence" showing how Mikedo's video was a forgery. This proved sufficient for most Crew to drop their questions about the rumors. The civilians clearly hadn't been as willing to accept those lies. Zax looked over at the Boss. The man seemed to be ignoring how the Omegas' deception was being exposed and continued to stare at the wall opposite where he sat.

"We know they're out there somewhere. Unfortunately, we have no way of knowing where this new human homeworld might be. Do we ignore their existence and continue stumbling forward to serve our hopeless Mission, or do we take decisive action to find these other humans and seek refuge from our dying Ship? A handful of Omegas tried to decide for us, but I'm here today to say we reject their authority in this critical matter. We're going to find the humans who built the spacecraft you see on your screen!

"Much to the chagrin of the Captain, the Flight Boss, and all of the other Omegas who run the Ship, I am not stupid enough to believe that just wishing for these humans to appear will allow us to find them. The odds of us just stumbling across these other humans are infinitesimal given how we've seen evidence of their existence once in five thousand years. No—what we need is a strategy to give

ourselves the best chance of finding them and we believe we've got just such a plan.

"Starting today we will work our way backwards to visit the colonies the Ship has established in the last five thousand years. Each of these outposts represents a shining beacon we hope may have attracted the attention of these mysterious humans. Our goal is to find additional evidence along this path which will point us to where these humans are originating from. Ideally, these humans will have made contact with some of our colonists and may even be living alongside them.

"What happens if we don't cross paths with these humans as we retrace our steps? Well, there's one last place where we may find evidence of who they are and where they may be. If all else fails, we will return to the very beginning of this Ship's journey—Earth."

The image of the human fighter was replaced by an image of Earth. It remained *by far* the most beautiful and hospitable of all the planets the Ship had ever encountered. Humanity had come of age swimming in its blue oceans and gazing up at its white wispy clouds, and it seemed fitting to think the Ship might soon return. Zax knew in his heart the planet was dead and it was a foolish dream as a final destination, and yet deep in his marrow he felt a yearning for *home* at the notion he might see that lonely blue marble with his own two eyes. After letting

Earth's image soak in for a while, the voice spoke again with increased vehemence.

"The Omegas made their decision to ignore the existence of other humans and press forward. We do not expect them to easily accept we have now chosen otherwise. We will help them to do so today. The Captain wants you to believe this is a ragtag group of civilians who will piss themselves out of fear when the first Marine in ChamWare appears out of thin air. We are not. We are half a million strong and we are prepared!"

There was a collective gasp in the compartment as each member of the Crew envisioned five hundred thousand berserk civilians. There was no doubt the Marines were well-armed and wildly powerful, but with ten to one odds in their favor the civilians might stand a chance. And if they already had 5% of the civilian population engaged, Zax couldn't help but wonder what would stop them from enlisting the other 95% and making those odds two hundred to one. Human history was chock full of insurgents who overcame great disparities in weaponry to win their cause.

"The past year has not been full of random riots. Each and every activity has been part of a master plan and prepared us for today. We don't want to harm anyone. We're not trying to take the Ship away from the Crew. We believe you're still the best people available to support our new goal of finding these other humans. We don't believe your

leadership is working towards the best interests of all the Ship's inhabitants, however, so we're going to help them see the error of their ways. Once they accept our plans, we're prepared to return most aspects of life back to what they were just a short time ago. This is not a mutiny. We're not going to send all of the Crew out an airlock. Unless you force us to."

The voice paused for a long moment to let those final words sink in.

"That's all for now. To those civilians not already involved, go back to your quarters. If we need your help, we'll call for you. To the Crew who are not already held captive by my teams, I implore you to put down your arms and return to your quarters as well. We've disabled the Tube system, so, unfortunately, you'll have to live like a civilian today and just walk.

"Captain—please hear me clearly. You've already lost control of the Ship and there's no need for any additional lives to be lost proving me right. I'll report back once we've finalized our takeover and gotten commitment from the Omegas to move forward with our plans."

The screens did not fade to black as usual after newsvids but instead displayed the image of the human fightercraft. Zax looked at the Flight Boss and saw a smirk on his face. Even with his current situation, the Omega seemed to doubt the notion he had truly lost control of his Ship. The irony was not lost on Zax that he how sat captive alongside the man who was a prime target of this revolution—a revolution which Zax himself instigated a year ago when he revealed the existence of other humans.

CHAPTER TEN

You can help them.

T he final words of the civilian's speech still lingered in the air when Rege spoke.

"All of you from Engineering should sit tight except the cadet. The Engineering cadet, along with the other two cadets, stand up. You get up as well, Mr. Flight Boss. And your little Marine too. I hate to break up our nice party here, but things will be more manageable if we get a few people separated."

Rege nodded in the direction of the burly civilian, and the man jabbed his blaster into Aleron's back to get him moving. Kalare fell into line behind Aleron and Zax followed immediately behind her. They exited the compartment and after a few secs of walking down the passageway, Zax turned to check behind him. He received a whack between the eyes from the butt of a blaster for his trouble.

"Eyes front!"

Zax followed the instruction and swiveled his head back. His eyes watered from pain, but he had seen what he wanted to. The giant civilian at the head of their column was joined by three others. One walked directly behind Zax, one was behind the Boss with his rifle pointed at the man's back, and the third trailed Bailee. The civilians appeared well-trained as they not only kept a tight formation but also left enough of a gap between the prisoners so they could react to sudden movements. Any action on the part of the Crew, especially while their hands remained bound, would most likely end with all of them shot dead.

After a couple of turns down the passageway, the civilian at the front stopped and gestured towards a hatch.

"Let's keep the Boss and whitey in here. I want the three of you to stand guard outside the compartment once you get them locked in. I can handle the kids on my own. Keep an eye on that Marine. He looks like a tricky one. If he gives you any grief, come get me and I'll happily take care of him for you."

The sergeant's suppressed rage turned his face an even deeper shade of crimson once he was called "whitey" and shoved towards the hatch by a blaster to the back.

Zax turned to follow Kalare and Aleron while the burly civilian took up the rear to herd the three cadets by himself. They walked for a few mins and made a left turn and then a right and then one more left. Along the way, they passed at least twelve more armed civilians who walked in twos and threes. All of them looked disciplined and purposeful to Zax. Eventually, their captor called for a halt in front of a compartment. He opened the hatch, pushed Aleron in, and then stood aside and gestured for Kalare and Zax to follow.

"You three get comfortable. You're gonna be here for quite a while as I don't see any reason we'll require you. We have more than enough Engineering Crew to get what we need."

The tone of the last sentence left sinking a feeling in the pit of Zax's stomach. During the walk he had obsessed about how effective their collars would be as torture devices and feared for the fate of the Crew who remained in the Engineering command center. The civilian began to leave and Kalare spoke up.

"Hey—I need to visit the head something fierce! Hey! Come on, don't go. Please!"

The civilian didn't stop walking but looked back over his shoulder and replied, "Hold on. I'll be right back."

He returned a moment later holding a bucket which he ceremoniously placed in the corner of the room and then gestured at with a sarcastic flourish. "Your throne awaits, ma'am. Turn around."

Kalare turned her back to the civilian who pulled a blade out of his boot and went to work on the bindings that held her hands.

"That's my blaster you feel in your back. I've got a real itchy trigger finger so don't think about trying anything cute." Once he had her hands freed, the civilian quickly backed out of reach towards the compartment hatch. "I'm going to leave now."

Kalare spoke out again. "Wait! You said we're going to be in here for a while. What happens if one of them needs to go?"

"You can help them."

"Ewww, no way! Come on. You're just going to lock us in here anyways. Cut their bindings too in case one of them needs to take a leak. No way I'm touching their junk! You're easily twice as big as any of us, plus you've got the blaster. Are you really that afraid of three kids you need to leave us tied up?"

The civilian appeared on the verge of ignoring Kalare's pleas but then decided otherwise. He raised his blaster to the ready position and made exaggerated motions to show he was aimed at Kalare and prepared to pull the trigger. He slid the blade across the floor towards her.

"OK, you've charmed me. Cut their bindings as well, but if you so much as twitch an eye while doing so, all three of you are dead. I'm not supposed to kill anyone, but self-defense is self-defense."

Zax turned his back to Kalare and a moment later was relieved to feel his bindings removed and circulation returning in his hands. He was stepping away from Kalare so Aleron could approach when he noticed the hair on the back of his neck stand up and his body slide into weightlessness. Zax was about to identify the familiar cause of the sensations when the room faded to black and he was unconscious...

...until he awoke what felt like an instant later and completed his thought. The Captain had engaged an FTL jump without warning. The three bells had woken Zax, which meant that gravity would return in less than one min. Zax quickly looked around. The cadets as well as the massive civilian were each floating in the zero-g which accompanied every FTL jump. Zax was the most alert of the Crew, but Kalare was almost fully conscious and Aleron wasn't too far behind. The civilian remained out cold. This disparity was to be expected given how much conditioning the Crew received to help them react to the three bells and return quickly from the depths of the unconsciousness that remained an unsolved side effect of the FTL engine.

Zax's breakfast had left his stomach while he was unconscious and now danced in the air as well. He was more than a year removed from being Plugged in, and the medics had still not managed the proper calibration to prevent him from puking each time the Ship engaged the FTL engine. Zax had suffered from this malady for most of his life and had been long promised that getting his Plug would provide the cure, but he continued to earn the nickname "Puke Boy" which Aleron had bestowed upon him. He typically arranged his eating plans to avoid a full stomach before a jump, but of course this one was unplanned and his stomach hadn't yet fully digested breakfast.

While observing the remains of his breakfast, Zax spotted something critical. The civilian had dropped his blaster and it hung in the air between them—up for grabs. This must have been what the Captain intended by engaging the jump. Zax pictured Crew and Marines all around the Ship being presented with similar opportunities where their superior FTL training would allow them to regain the upper hand if they acted quickly enough.

The complication was that Zax floated so far from any solid surface he was unable to push off and affect his movement. He stretched his legs until his toes barely reached the bulkhead. It wasn't much leverage, but he established enough contact to impart the tiniest bit of momentum and directed his body towards the blaster in a slow glide.

Zax kept an eye on the civilian as he floated for the weapon and was dismayed to see him return to consciousness scant secs later. The hulking man regained situational awareness almost immediately, and a wicked smile spread across his face as he realized what Zax was attempting. The civilian had a huge advantage over Zax because he was floating right up against the bulkhead. He quickly reoriented himself, coiled his full body to leverage his considerable strength, and pushed off towards the blaster.

Even with a significant head start, Zax realized immediately the civilian's acceleration advantage would be insurmountable in their zero-g race for the weapon. Physics often picked the most inopportune time to rear its head. Zax watched hopelessly as the civilian closed the distance first and wrapped his fingertips around the blaster's barrel.

The man was reorienting the blaster in his hands to grip it properly when the gravity generator reengaged. Zax cartwheeled to the ground and was winded as his weight returned and his full mass slammed into first his shoulder and then his back. Even as he saw stars from the impact, Zax maintained enough of his senses to hear the blaster clang out of the civilian's grasp and rattle across the deck. It came to rest a few meters away, and Zax scuttled for it on his hands and knees.

Zax grabbed the butt of the blaster and rolled over to face the civilian as he desperately fumbled to aim and pull the trigger. The man recovered from his own rough fall and charged at full speed. He launched himself at Zax in an effort to pin the blaster uselessly between them before he could fire.

The force of the flying tackle would have knocked Zax out cold were it not for the fact the civilian's foot slipped at the last instant (in a pile of half-digested eggs) and sent him slightly off target.

Even so, Zax was slammed against the bulkhead with much of the man's weight on top of him. He attempted to scramble out from under the civilian's sprawl, but the man was double his mass and quickly pulled Zax back under him.

The civilian's enormous hands easily encircled Zax's throat and squeezed. Zax fought for his life, but it was no contest given the size differential. Even with all of the panicked strength Zax could muster, his desperate flailing against the man's arms had no effect. The civilian's sadistic grin intensified and sweat beaded and dripped off his massive bald head. His vision began to fade and Zax was on the verge of blacking out when the man suddenly went wide-eyed. The tip of a blade appeared below his chin, and he released Zax's neck to clutch desperately at his own. The civilian gagged on the blood which spurted out of his mouth until the blade turned 90 degrees and the man's eyes went vacant. He keeled over and hit the deck with a lifeless thud.

The last thing Zax saw before passing out was Kalare standing over the burly corpse with blood dripping off the knife in her hand.

CHAPTER ELEVEN

I agree with Aleron.

For the second time that morning, Zax was brought back to consciousness by a slap to his face. He opened his eyes and basked in Kalare's warm smile for a moment before he was overwhelmed with the urge to cough. The uncontrollable spasms triggered by having his throat nearly crushed ended with Zax retching the final remnants of his breakfast on to the deck next to the dead civilian.

"Th...than...thank you," he managed to gasp. "Wh...what took you so long?"

"Sorry, Zax. I'm really sorry. I know that was close, and I can only imagine how scary it was for you. It looked like that guy just about had you strangled? Am I right? Were you almost dead? Wow, that must have been scary. That guy was huge!" Kalare looked at all the blood pooling around the dead civilian and giggled for a couple of secs before continuing. "I watched you floating for the blaster and wanted to help, but when the gravity came back I landed on my head and was in a daze. Not all of us have the well-practiced zero-g capabilities of Puke Boy! Hah! Well, anyways, my head cleared and I could see he was on top of you, but I didn't think I had a chance against him without a weapon. I couldn't get at the blaster because it was sandwiched between the two of you. I looked around for the knife, but it had slid under a workstation and I wasn't able to reach it at first. Of course, Captain Clueless over there just sat and whimpered the entire time."

Kalare's monologue provided Zax with sufficient time to recover. Her last comment reminded him that Aleron was with them, and he looked over to find the boy in the corner quietly sobbing. The cadet's hands were still bound so Zax stood, grabbed the blade off the deck where Kalare had dropped it, and used the civilian's pants to wipe off the worst of the blood. After he freed Aleron's hands, Zax helped the boy to his feet. Being rescued by the frequent target of his abuse was clearly unpalatable for Aleron. He brushed aside Zax's assistance and turned away to use his freed hands to wipe the remains of tears from his face.

Kalare had the presence of mind to not only pick up the blaster but also secure the compartment hatch shut while he worked to free Aleron. They were lucky none of the roving groups of civilians had passed the open hatch in the middle of their struggles. Zax looked at Kalare, then back towards Aleron, and finally back to Kalare before speaking.

"Now what?"

No one spoke for a min as they each considered the question. Aleron broke the silence.

"We wait here, of course! We've got the hatch locked and there's a possibility no one even knows we're in here. You saw all those civilians roaming around out there. There's no chance of us making it far if we try to get anywhere else. Besides, we just managed to take care of this monster, so you've got to think other Crew, especially the Marines, have taken care of this mess. It won't be much longer, I bet, before the Captain is on the vidscreen letting us know this whole damn thing is over."

Zax was forming a snide comment about the "we" in Aleron's description of the dead civilian when Kalare jumped in first.

"No. They know we're in here. He didn't bring us to this compartment randomly. He knew exactly where he was going. We don't know what he was supposed to do after securing us in here. He clearly didn't think we posed any threat since he wasn't going to stick around and guard the compartment. They might have already missed him and sent more goons here looking for him."

Aleron and Kalare looked to Zax as the tiebreaker. He took a few deep breaths and then spoke.

"I agree with Aleron." Zax felt a pang of deep regret when Kalare deflated in response to his statement, but pushed onwards. "I can't believe I'm saying this, but I think he's right. That FTL jump was brilliant in allowing *you and me, Kalare,* to take care of this idiot. I've got to think the Marines and Crew throughout the Ship have cut up the rest of these jokers and they just haven't had a moment to tell us it's over yet. Wait—the vidscreens are coming back online. I bet this is the Captain now."

They all expectantly faced the compartment's screen as the image of the human fighter pixelated and scrambled. It was replaced not with the Captain's face but instead cycled through images showing various compartments which appeared to have been torn apart by bomb blasts. Bloodied and dismembered bodies, civilian and Crew alike, dominated the pictures. Zax and Kalare both gasped when Flight Ops, with its unique dual panoramas, appeared on the screen. Zax recognized a few of the dead Crew as people he had worked with previously and imagined that Kalare must know all of them. Each image featured large numbers of dead Marines with their heavy battle armor mangled and shattered. The same voice from the earlier announcement started to speak as the bloody images continued to cycle.

"I regret to inform everyone that your Captain made a very poor choice. She clearly didn't believe me when I said she had lost control of the Ship and decided to put my assertion to the test with her ill-advised FTL jump. I can only assume her intent was to allow Marines to retake certain compartments. The images you are watching were taken from Flight Ops, Primary Grav Control, and Primary Life Support among others. My teams who earlier took command of critical compartments such as these came prepared with explosives. Members of each team have detonators biologically implanted which will trigger their bombs if that team member dies or is no longer within close proximity of their assigned device. Of course, team members can also choose to detonate manually if they feel they are under threat and want to neutralize the compartment rather than allow the Crew to regain control."

Zax thought back to the unidentified cases he had seen arranged around Engineering Control after the civilians arrived. He imagined they were close enough to hear the blast if those were indeed bombs and Engineering had suffered the same fate as Flight Ops, but it was impossible to know for certain. He focused back on the screen as the woman continued.

"Captain—I implore you to understand you are no longer in charge. We are. Do not attempt anything like this again. Acknowledge my attempts to communicate with you directly. We can resolve this situation without further loss of life or the Ship's

operational capacity, but only if you respond to my attempts to hail you and discuss the terms of your surrender."

The voice paused for a moment and then returned.

"I'm pleased to announce we've finally established communication with the Bridge. I'm not yet speaking with the Captain, but I hope to do so as soon as she's ready to work together to resolve this matter. In the meantime, I reiterate my call for all Crew to drop your arms and return to your quarters. There's no need for any more of you to die today than already have."

CHAPTER TWELVE

Give me the blaster!

Kalare spoke as soon as the vidscreen faded back to the image of the human fighter.

"OK, that settles it. We've got to get out of here now!"

Aleron seemed dumbfounded. "Are you crazy? You heard her. They've got full control and are talking to the Bridge right now. The Captain will agree to whatever they want and end this any min. Why do you want to risk running into trigger-happy civilians and getting ourselves killed?"

"You're delusional if you think the Captain is going to surrender, Aleron." Kalare's voice became more strident. "I don't know the woman, but I damn well know the Flight Boss, and they're cut from the same cloth. That man would sooner cut off the oxygen supply and kill everyone on board before he would give in to a civilian's demands. In fact, we're all probably lucky that Primary Life Support got blown up and now it will be more challenging for the Omegas to do exactly that. We've got to get out of here and find a safer place to be before all hell breaks loose. You know I'm right, Zax, tell him!"

Zax had intended to back Aleron once again, but Kalare's observations about the Flight Boss hit their mark. He certainly hadn't spent as much time with the man as she had, but he had even greater reason to believe the man was ruthless enough to consider the deaths of nearly all ten million aboard the Ship a small price to pay if it ended the uprising. If that's how the Boss would solve the problem, it seemed a safe bet to assume the Captain would act similarly.

"Kalare's right, Aleron. We've got to get out of here. Engineering is clearly a hotspot for anyone trying to wrest control of the Ship and we're likely to get shot or blown up if we stick around here. We'll have a greater chance if the three of us stick together, though, so please come with us."

That last bit was painful for Zax to utter, but he believed it to be true and choked it out regardless. He watched as Aleron silently weighed his options.

"Fine—I'll stick with you two oxygen thieves, but I want the blaster."

Kalare guffawed and her response instantly triggered a change in Aleron's demeanor. He stood tall and puffed out his chest as he walked menacingly towards her with his arm reaching for the weapon. He hadn't quite achieved the height and mass of his (thankfully Culled) mentor Cyrus, but he towered over both Kalare and Zax and was clearly prepared to leverage his size advantage if violence was required. As he approached her, he bellowed, "Give me the blaster!"

Kalare's posture shifted from defiance to acquiescence as she moved the weapon towards Aleron's outstretched hand. The boy was half a stride away from her and a satisfied grin was forming on his lips when Kalare's weight shifted to her back leg and her forward foot shot off the deck and connected with his testicles. Aleron emitted no sound as he crashed to the deck in the fetal position. Kalare turned to Zax and spoke as if nothing had happened.

"Do you have any ideas about where we should go?"

Zax pondered alternatives for a moment, but he couldn't think of anything better than the first thought which had come to mind. "Waste Systems. It's not that far, and I know how we can reach it through maintenance tunnels rather than the main passageways. I can't imagine the civilians care enough about sewage to send anyone there to take it over."

Kalare nodded in agreement. "Perfect." She paused and appeared contemplative for a moment before speaking again. "I think we should first figure out how to free the Boss and Bailee and take them with us."

"What? No way! It's bad enough we have to deal with Aleron. What makes you think I want to put my neck on the line trying to save that man?"

Kalare sighed. "Trust me, Zax, I'm not about to throw away my life trying to help the Flight Boss out of any sense of duty or anything silly like that. But think about it. Won't we stand a much better chance of staying alive if we have a little more help than Captain Clueless here? Can you think of anyone better than Bailee to have by our side in the middle of all this craziness?"

Zax hated to admit it, but Kalare was right. Connecting with the Marine would increase their odds of survival substantially and, unfortunately, getting access to him meant throwing their fate in with that of the Boss as well. Zax tried to find solace in the possibility they'd get caught in a firefight along the way and he might be able to witness the Boss get killed by a civilian.

As Aleron continued to writhe on the deck, Zax visualized the maintenance tunnels and crawlspaces he had studied months earlier. His ability to vividly recall the details of imagery like maps and schematics had served Zax well during his time as a cadet, but this was the first time he'd rely on it in a truly life or death situation.

"OK. This can work. It would be so much easier and safer if we could just access the crawlspace directly above us, but our Plugs are blocked by these damn collars and I can't release the lock on the hatch. There's an access port around the corner though that has biometric controls. I can get us in there, and it connects with a shaft that will put us into the crawlspace above the compartment where they put Bailee and the Boss. *If* they are still in there, and *if* the guards are still outside, we can use the manual override for the hatch from the crawlspace to get them out."

Kalare smiled at Zax before looking down at Aleron who remained on the deck grasping his crotch. Her grin widened as she gave him another (reasonably light) kick to get his attention. "Quit your sniveling and get your butt up. We're getting out of here."

CHAPTER THIRTEEN

We have to deliver a message.

Kalare led the way out of the compartment with the blaster hidden under her shirt in the small of her back. Aleron shambled along directly behind her. Zax brought up the rear once he removed the sheath from the dead civilian's boot and secured the blade in his own.

Zax was most worried about the first fifty meters of the trip. They would be totally exposed as they made their way from the compartment to the access port for the maintenance tunnels. If they ran into any civilians, their plan was to pass themselves off as random cadets desperately trying to make their way back to their quarters, but Zax didn't hold out much hope that would work.

They approached a T-junction where they needed to turn left when suddenly Aleron sprang to life and grabbed a fistful of Kalare's shirt. He dragged her backwards and pushed her up tight against a closed hatch while using his other hand to pull Zax in alongside them. It seemed like the bully was making his play to reestablish dominance until Zax heard voices and footsteps approach from arround the corner. He held his breath and waited until a group of three civilians walked past in the connecting passageway without looking their way.

The voices faded and eventually Aleron released his grip and backed away from Kalare and Zax with a smirk. "Who's Captain Clueless now?"

Kalare straightened her shirt and glared at Aleron. "I might have been able to hear them a little more easily if I wasn't so distracted by how slowly you were moving your sorry carcass." Her expression softened a bit. "But thank you—that would not have been good to run straight into that group." She held up her hand to signal quiet and then peeked around the corner until she was satisfied the next passageway was now empty.

They walked the last ten meters without incident and the three cadets were soon through the access port into a world entirely unknown to almost everyone who called the Ship home. The network of maintenance tunnels was a motley collection—some were the same size and build quality as the main passageways while others were nothing but crawlspaces roughly hewn into the mammoth asteroid that formed the foundation of the Ship. Civilians were not allowed unescorted access, and most Crew never bothered requesting the security credentials needed to open its hatches and access ports. The tunnels were universally considered a warren best left to those with the lowest Leaderboard rankings, so Zax had never encountered another person during his travels within them.

Frequent usage of the tunnel system made life in Waste Systems more efficient which is what inspired Zax to study and explore it in the first place. Thankfully his eidetic memory meant prior glances at the schematics for Engineering were sufficient for him to recall how its maintenance network was laid out as well. Zax confidently led the other two cadets through seemingly random twists and turns until he stopped them at the base of a ladder and spoke.

"This goes into the crawlspace above the compartment where the Boss and Bailee are being held. I want you two to wait here with the blaster. If you hear any commotion, I want you to run. I know you don't have a clue where you're going, but it doesn't matter. Just run. Better to be lost in the tunnels than dead from the civilians. Any exterior hatch you find will have a manual override which will let you exit the system. Be careful, though. If you let a hatch shut behind you, you'll be stuck wherever you exited because neither of you has the access credentials to get back into the tunnels."

Aleron leaned against the wall and pouted. The bully clearly didn't appreciate being stuck in a situation where Zax's low Leaderboard status actually provided the advantage which left him in charge. Kalare appraised Zax with a worried expression. She took a deep breath and opened her mouth in the fashion which usually kicked off a monologue, but then she appeared to think better of it and turned away. When she looked back, she graced Zax with a tight smile and simply wished him luck.

The journey through the crawlspace was uneventful. Zax stopped to listen at each hatch he passed, but every compartment below was empty until he came to the one which held the Boss and Sergeant Bailee. He sat quietly to ascertain whether the two men were by themselves inside the compartment or if they were being more closely guarded. He couldn't make out their words but after a few mins had only heard their two voices. Civilian guards wouldn't be likely to let them carry on a conversation for so long uninterrupted and Zax hoped the lack of unknown voices meant they must be alone. There was no other way to find out for certain, so Zax took a deep breath, triggered the manual override, and lifted the hatch.

The utter confusion on the gruff Marine's face when he saw Zax's head pop down from the overhead was priceless. The Flight Boss was speaking with his back to the hatch, and it took him an extra moment to react to the sergeant's expression and follow his eyes up to the hatch opening. Once he made eye contact with Zax, however, the Boss didn't waste any additional time before addressing him in a forceful whisper.

"You're not quite the rescue party I was hoping for, but I suppose you're not entirely worthless. Get down here and get our hands loose!"

Zax was tempted to shut the hatch and leave the obnoxious Omega to whatever fate the civilians had in mind for him, but then he thought about Kalare waiting back in the tunnel counting on Bailee's assistance. He shimmied out of the hatch and lowered himself down slowly so as to land on the deck as quietly as possible. He cut the binds holding the Flight Boss's hands and then freed Sergeant Bailee. There was something about the expression on the Marine's face and the way he carried his body that made Zax think something was wrong, but the Boss started hissing commands before Zax could ask any questions.

"I'll boost you up first, Zax, and then Bailee. You can both help me climb up. From down here the hatch looks just like every other panel in the overhead so if we can manage to do this without moving any equipment underneath then just maybe these idiot civilians won't be smart enough to figure out where we went."

Without waiting for any form of acknowledgement, the Flight Boss grabbed Zax and roughly heaved him up to the hatch. He almost clambered back into the crawlspace, but then he lost his grip and slid back out. Only the outstretched arms of the Boss prevented Zax from crashing to the deck. The officer slammed him down onto his feet and then spun Zax around to look in his eyes.

"Boy—you need to do this right and you need to do it *now*! If you screw this up, I will kill you with my bare hands and stand on your lifeless corpse to boost myself up into that hatch."

Zax certainly hadn't expected much in the way of gratitude from the Boss, but even so he was taken aback by the way the man was treating him. Before he could say a word, he was once again spun around and launched up towards the hatch. This time, he established a firm grip and pulled himself into the crawlspace. Zax turned around and poked his torso back out with his arms outstretched to assist Bailee. The Marine was putting a foot onto the Boss's interlocked fingers for a lift up but shook off Zax's offer of assistance.

"No—back up and let me grip it myself. If I struggle, then grab the back of my shirt and pull me in."

It struck Zax as odd that the Marine doubted his ability to perform the same maneuver which Zax had just done, but he moved away from the hatch. A moment later the sergeant's left hand was inside the hatch. Zax looked down and saw the man's right arm hung limply by his side. The man's face was deep crimson from exertion as he tried to power himself up into the hatch with nothing more than the strength of one hand's fingertips. Zax grabbed two fistfuls of Bailee's shirt and after a few moments of furious struggle was able to help the Marine into the crawlspace.

Once the sergeant was settled, they next turned to the Flight Boss. This would be the trickiest maneuver as the officer would have nothing but his own strength plus whatever assistance Zax and Bailee could provide from above to climb in. They each extended one arm and after taking a few steps backwards the Omega got a running start and jumped high enough for them to get a hold of him. Even though Bailee was doing most of the heavy lifting, Zax felt himself losing his tenuous grip on the Boss's arm. He held on for dear life after the admonition he had received earlier, and they successfully wrangled the man in.

Bailee secured the hatch shut, and then Zax led the way through the crawlspace back to the ladder. Zax called out to Kalare as they got close to be sure she wouldn't get nervous and start blindly shooting at the noise of their approach. A moment later the five Crew stood in a circle and appraised each other silently until the Boss spoke.

"Getting into the maintenance tunnels was a great idea, Kalare. Where were you planning to go if you hadn't been able to link up with us?"

"It was actually Zax's plan, sir. You should hear it from him."

The Boss appeared thoroughly disappointed with Kalare's response but turned his attention to Zax and gestured for him to speak.

"Sir—I've been working in Waste Systems since I left Flight Ops, which is how I got familiar with the maintenance network in the first place. It's not that far away and we can get there using the tunnels exclusively. I was thinking sewage treatment is probably the last place where the civilians will have bothered sending anyone."

The Boss turned away to consider the plan. The muscles in the man's cheeks twitched as his teeth sought the unlit cigar which would normally be chomped upon as part of his thought process. After a couple of secs, he turned back and addressed the group.

"That's a surprisingly good idea, Zax. I suppose creativity goes hand in hand with that active imagination of yours. There's something critical we need to do first. We have to deliver a message." The Boss paused for a moment to look at Sergeant Bailee who nodded agreement. "To the Chief Engineer."

CHAPTER FOURTEEN

Why did you do that?

T he Flight Boss didn't allow the cadets so much as a sec to recover from the shock of his words. They had just risked their lives to free the Boss from the civilians, and now the man was asking them to turn around and head back towards the biggest group of insurgents in their immediate vicinity—the ones in Engineering Control. The group who almost certainly had rigged the compartment with sufficient explosives to kill all of its occupants along with anyone else nearby. The Omega laid out his plan, and it was clear from his posture and tone there was no room for question or suggestions.

Zax led the way as the five of them double-timed through the tunnels until they came to a path the cadets had passed by earlier. This time, they turned and followed the new passage until they reached a different ladder which would access a different crawlspace and eventually run above Engineering Control. Sergeant Bailee held his hand out to Kalare for the blaster, and she heeded the unspoken request without hesitation. The Marine tucked the weapon into his waistband to free up his only functional arm and then gestured for Zax to lead the way up the ladder.

The plan was for the Boss to remain behind with Kalare and Aleron while Zax led Bailee through the crawlspace to Engineering Control. The Marine would then pop his head out of the hatch and deliver whatever message the Boss felt was so critical he was willing to risk all of their lives to deliver it. Zax could not imagine anything important enough to delay hightailing it over to the relative safety of Waste Systems, but kept that counsel to himself.

Zax crawled towards their destination. He turned back after ten meters and saw how much Bailee was struggling to keep up. The man winced each time he was forced to balance his weight on his right arm. Zax queried the Marine.

"What happened to your arm, Sergeant?"

"A little misadventure with zero-g after that surprise FTL Transit. It was pretty challenging to maneuver with my hands bound behind my back, and I ended up landing funny when the grav-gen kicked in. I heard a good *crack* so I'm pretty confident it snapped my collarbone. I can use the arm a little, but it hurts like hell."

"Can you share what message is so important the Boss is sending a cadet and a seriously wounded Marine back into the thick of armed civilians to try to deliver it?"

"No. Let's get moving, cadet."

"Yes, Sergeant."

Zax started crawling again, and after a few mins they approached the first hatch in the vicinity of Engineering Control. They stopped for a moment to eavesdrop on the compartment below. Numerous voices spoke at full volume. It was impossible to know for certain whether it was Crew or civilians, but Zax couldn't imagine a group of Crew sounding so calm and cavalier in this situation and assumed it must be a large group of renegades. A similar number of voices emanated from the second compartment they passed and Zax's spirits plummeted even further. It was clear there were now far more insurgents in the area. Zax pressed onwards, as he had no choice in the matter, and they soon reached their destination. He stopped at the appropriate hatch and signaled to the Marine that they had arrived.

They paused to listen. There were fewer discussions in the compartment below than the others they had passed, but there was one voice which Zax easily recognized. Rege, the leader of the civilians who had captured Engineering Control, was doing most of the talking. Zax took a deep breath in a hopeless attempt to calm his thundering heart as the Marine primed his blaster. Zax assumed the man wanted to be prepared to defend them in case a civilian managed to react quickly and got off some shots while the sergeant was still delivering his message.

"Zax," the Marine whispered, "here's what I need you to do. It's a big compartment, and we aren't going to have a lot of time. We're going to surprise them by popping out of the overhead, but all hell's going to break loose faster than you know it. I need to get eyes on the Chief Engineer as fast as possible, so we need to cover the whole compartment simultaneously. I want you to look to your left once the hatch opens and I'll look to your right. We'll call your half of the compartment zero to 180 degrees and you should call out the Chief's position by degree if you spot her first. OK?"

Zax nodded agreement and took another exaggeratedly deep breath. The sergeant reached for the hatch's manual override with his injured arm and mouthed a silent countdown from five. As soon as the hatch flew open, Zax popped his head down and scanned his portion of the compartment.

Everything looked pretty much the same as when they had left, though the bodies of two additional Crew had joined the pile of dead. Zax didn't allow himself to dwell on how mangled one of the new corpses was and instead focused on spotting the Chief Engineer.

"Sergeant—120 degrees!"

Two things happened immediately after Zax yelled the words. Rege looked up at the open hatch with a look of complete disbelief, and Bailee's blaster went off right next to Zax's ear. His eyes closed involuntarily in response to being so close to a weapon discharge, but not before Zax saw the Marine's shot find its target and the Chief Engineer's head disappear in a shower of bloody mist.

Before Zax could even think to react, the sergeant pulled him violently out of the opening, slammed the hatch shut, and engaged the lock. The compartment below exploded into a cacophony of blaster shots which Zax feared would shred the crawlspace at any moment.

"Move cadet! They can't penetrate the overhead with the blasters they had earlier, but if their reinforcements brought heavier weapons, we might be in trouble."

Zax saw the Marine's lips moving but barely heard his words. He wanted to move, but his ears rang too loudly and he was unable to focus his eyes. He closed them for what seemed to be a moment, but when he opened them he recognized how he'd been dragged by the Marine at least 15 meters away from the hatch. The agony on the sergeant's face was plain as he used his injured arm to crawl and pulled Zax's mass with the other one. Zax swatted the Marine's hand away and moved under his own power until they reached the ladder which led to the others.

His initial shock subsided by the time Zax descended the ladder. When he came face to face with the Boss, it had been replaced with enough rage that he exploded at the Omega.

"We didn't deliver any message—you had him kill the Chief Engineer! Why did you do that? Why did I risk my life just so you could take the Chief's?"

"Watch yourself, cadet. The rules about insubordination don't get suspended just because we're under attack. When I feel the need to explain myself, I'll let you know. Until then, I need you to quit squawking and get us the hell out of here."

Zax considered a couple of inappropriate replies, but the threat in the Boss's tone was even more pronounced than the man's words. He controlled himself until the urge to speak passed. He stomped down the tunnel and brushed past the idiotically grinning Aleron. Even when his own life was in danger, that tool still managed to find pleasure in Zax's troubles.

Kalare caught up to him a moment later and put a hand on Zax's shoulder to silently commiserate. He swatted it away.

"Get back there with *your mentor* and leave me alone. At least there can be no argument about whether he was responsible for *this* murder!"

CHAPTER FIFTEEN

With all due respect, sir, we shouldn't split up.

The group trailed Zax in silence as he led them towards the tunnels which connected with Waste Systems. His body ran on autopilot while his brain spun about what he had just been part of. Try as he might, no valid reason came to mind as to why the Boss might want to kill the Chief. The additional dead bodies he had seen confirmed the civilians were using the collars and torturing the Crew, but Zax couldn't imagine their goals. Anything they might try to negatively impact the Ship from the Engineering compartment could be easily overridden by the Captain from the Bridge. He finally pushed the thoughts aside and chalked the woman's murder up as just more evidence of the Boss's callous insanity.

Zax dedicated his focus back to their journey and getting safely to Waste Systems. He expected at any moment to hear the clamor which would signal the civilians had forced their way into the maintenance network. The closest they got to this outcome was a loud commotion on the other side of one access port as they scurried past. Zax thought the racket might have included the hum of a drill being used in an attempt to force open the port, so he concluded a shift in route was in order.

At his next opportunity, Zax took a ladder down to the lowest level it connected with. He did the same at the next ladder and then once again when they encountered a third. At the completion of that last, lengthiest ladder descent the Boss called for a halt.

"Why are you bringing us so deep, cadet?"

"Sir—if the civilians break into the tunnel network, they will search for us around the levels where they know we were last active. Rather than make things easy for them, I figured we were better off dropping lower. I think we've gone deep enough now, though, and intend to bring us straight over to Waste Systems from here."

The Boss seemed pleasantly surprised and nodded his agreement with Zax's assessment. As he started walking again, Zax picked up the smell of sewage. He didn't know if the others noticed it as well, but the human nose is finely attuned to the scent of feces, and Zax's had always seemed to be even more sensitive than most. The odor provided a means of gauging their progress because it became more and more pronounced the closer they got to the treatment cavern deep below the Waste Systems control room. That vile compartment held the massive sewage processing vessels. Zax had visited once but hoped to never see it again.

The group finally reached a ladder, and Zax gazed up the towering shaft with gratitude. Their ascent would take them away from the treatment cavern and its stench of human waste. When they finally reached the top, he stepped aside and waited for everyone to catch up. Sergeant Bailee brought up the rear, and Zax almost gasped when he saw the physical distress the Marine appeared to be in after his one-armed climb. He was trying to find the courage to suggest a rest break when his thoughts were interrupted by the Boss.

"Cadet—I want you and me to scout up ahead before we go further. This seems like as good a place as any for the others to wait behind for us."

Zax was gratified for Bailee's opportunity to rest, but Kalare seemed agitated by the plan and voiced her concerns.

"With all due respect, sir, we shouldn't split up. We don't know what's going on in this section, and it seems like a bad idea for us to not stay together."

The officer smiled benevolently at Kalare as he replied.

"The lack of knowledge you mention is exactly the rationale for us to split up. Rather than rush all five of us into a potential danger zone, it seems prudent to get a sense of what we might be walking into. Zax and I will press ahead to see if there is any civilian activity outside of the tunnel network along our route."

Zax agreed with Kalare's assessment but knew any hesitancy he might express would not be greeted anywhere near as patiently by the Boss. Zax gave her a wan smile as he walked past, and she returned a brighter one along with a pat on the shoulder for encouragement.

They had only walked a couple dozen meters when the Boss stopped and turned to Zax.

"I thought it was prudent for Bailee to have a few mins to recover from that climb. I knew he would resist the suggestion, so I thought a short scouting mission by the two of us would provide the excuse for him to rest. I'll call you a liar and whack you with some serious demerits if you let the Marine know I cut him some slack."

The Omega's wan smile and his tepid joke made it seem like he might be extending an offer of truce, but Zax didn't trust it to be genuine. He almost wished for the return of the Boss who had alternated between cruel and rude since Zax had set eyes on him a few hours ago. At least Zax knew where he stood with that man, versus whatever subterfuge the officer was likely disguising now with his faux humor.

"Is there a crawlspace that can get us above Waste Systems Control, Zax? It would be good to see if there are any unattended Crew in there as that would confirm the civilians hadn't bothered coming here."

"Yes, sir. Follow me."

Zax wasn't enthusiastic about being alone with the Boss for as long as it would take to scout out the control room and return but having a defined destination took some of the edge off his worry. They took advantage of every opportunity along their path to eavesdrop on the world outside the tunnels. There was not a sound to be heard outside any of the access ports, and once they got up into the overhead crawlspace, they heard nothing but silence in the compartments they passed. This was initially true of Waste Systems Control as well, but just before they turned to leave Zax heard Westerick call out and Salmea respond. The two officers spoke back and forth for a couple of mins without any other voices interjecting, so Zax concluded they were indeed alone and signaled for the Boss to head back out of the crawlspace.

"Sir—those voices we heard back at the hatch were Lieutenant Salmea and Major Westerick. She's my supervisor and he runs Waste Systems. I believe they're alone since we only heard the two of them speaking"

"I don't know her, but I'm familiar with him. What's your opinion of the Major, Zax?"

One look at the Boss's face made it clear to Zax that the man was testing him. He didn't know what answer was expected, but after a short deliberation decided that honesty was the best policy—within reason.

"The Major seems perfectly suited to run Waste Systems, sir."

The Flight Boss appraised Zax for a long moment and then broke into one of his hearty laughs before finally responding.

"Well said, cadet, well said. Let's get back to the rest of the team."

They walked for a few mins and were getting close to where they had left the others when Zax was startled by pounding on an access port as they walked past. The boss put his finger across his lips to signal silence and then motioned for them to double-time it the rest of the way. Zax turned the final corner and stopped short from the shock of discovering the junction where they had left the others was empty. The Boss almost collided with Zax but quickly recovered and voiced his disbelief.

"Where in the hell did they go?"

CHAPTER SIXTEEN

Where are we?

They searched the immediate vicinity, but there was no sign of Kalare or the others in the nearby tunnels. They wouldn't have wandered off within the labyrinthine maintenance network, so that suggested they had left the tunnels and gone into the main passageways. Zax worried about leaving the tunnels, particularly after they had just heard a ruckus a few mins ago, but feared losing track of Kalare far worse.

"Sir—I don't see what choice we have at this point. We've got to find them."

"We always have a choice, cadet, but we must be sure that even when we make the right choice we are making it for the right reasons. If you hadn't thrown away my offer of mentorship last year, you'd already be well familiar with that lesson. What are your reasons for seeking our companions?"

Just saying "Kalare" would not be an acceptable response in the Boss's eyes, even if it was honestly the sum total of Zax's motivation. He thought for a moment before answering.

"Because our tactical situation is far better when we are traveling with a Marine armed with a blaster, sir, even when said Marine is as injured as Sergeant Bailee."

"Exactly right, cadet, well done. One hundred credits. Now, let's head out the access port over here and see if we can find them."

Zax momentarily found himself flustered and didn't immediately follow behind the Boss. He had zero trust for the murderous Omega and desired nothing more than to abandon him to his fate in the tunnel network, but the man's praise triggered reward centers in Zax's brain which had been firmly wired by a lifetime of chasing career advancement. He tried to shake the feeling off but found it was difficult to do so. It was only one hundred credits, but having the Boss dole out *any* bonus in the middle of this disaster made Zax wonder what additional rewards might be in store if he successfully led the Omega to safety.

He had originally agreed to rescue the Boss primarily to make Kalare happy, but Zax now glimpsed how doing so could be his ticket back up the Leaderboard and out of the odorous hell of Waste Systems. They were in the middle of chaos right now, but there was no way the Marines would fail to overcome the civilian uprising and Zax had already learned how chaos sometimes created opportunity. A year ago the Boss had given him 8,000 credits for patching the panorama in Flight Ops during a battle. Wouldn't saving his life from rampaging civilians be worth some multiple of that?

But then Zax thought back to the fate of the Chief Engineer. The Boss ordering the murder of his fellow Omega was just another example of how he would stop at nothing to satisfy whatever schemes ran deep in his mind. The notion he might now turn around and make any meaningful contribution to Zax's career standing was absurd.

Zax set aside the foolish delusion and grounded himself back in the reality of his situation. Getting the Boss to safety was only valuable because it would get himself and Kalare to safety as well. At least, if they could find her and the others again. He ran to catch up and did so as the Boss stopped to listen at the access port.

"I don't hear anything out there, cadet. I'm going to open this just enough for you to peek your head out. If you see anyone you don't want to see, then pull yourself back immediately. That will be my signal to slam the hatch shut. If it's empty, then listen in for a min. If we don't hear or see anything, then let's go on through."

The Omega opened the hatch and Zax stuck his head out. A quick glance left and right proved the passageway to be empty as expected. Zax silently counted to sixty as he listened intently for any noise, but the area sounded as abandoned as it appeared. He stepped out into the bright light of the main passage and motioned for the Boss to follow.

"Where are we?"

Zax didn't hesitate as he knew the area well. "Compartment 51-F is around that corner, sir. If we head this way instead, it will put us on the path to reaching Waste Systems Control. I doubt Bailee and the others know exactly how to get there, but they knew it was our eventual destination. It seems like the most logical direction for us to head with the hope of finding them. It's actually faster in the tunnels, but I think we should stay in the main passageways and hope we run into them along the way."

"Agreed. Let's move out. Take it slow and quiet, cadet, so we don't give anyone a chance to hear us coming."

Zax led the way. At the hatch for each compartment off the passageway, they halted for a moment and listened before checking inside. At every turn and intersection of the passage, they paused and checked for noise beyond before poking their heads around for a quick scan. It made for extremely slow going but was the prudent approach when you never knew if you might turn a corner only to find a pack of rebels. What exactly they would do if they encountered civilians other than run or surrender, Zax had no clue.

Waste Systems was never a bustling hub of activity, but Zax found it eerie to see it so absolutely deserted. The civilian workers had clearly heeded the announcement to return to their quarters. Some literally dropped what they were doing as evidenced by the work materials scattered all around—a mess that was only exacerbated by the unplanned FTL. The Boss and Zax moved on as soon as they verified each new compartment was empty, but eventually the Omega broke the pattern.

"There's something about this compartment that seems odd, cadet. Keep watch outside while I check it more thoroughly."

Zax had no idea why this compartment struck the man as any more interesting than the others they had quickly checked and left, but he had long since stopped trying to understand the inner workings of the minds of Omegas. It would probably be easier to crack the mysteries of the FTL engine than to decipher why the Ship's most senior officers did the things they did. Zax kept his eyes scanning back and forth to check both ends of the passageway while he listened intently for the slightest noise. A min later the Boss returned shaking his head.

"Nothing. I thought there was something a little *too* random about the way the tools and such were scattered around the compartment, but I didn't see anything out of the ordinary. Let's get moving."

The next compartment appeared to be nothing but more of the same. Zax had turned to leave when he caught movement out of the corner of his eye. A shadow darted out of an impossibly small hiding place near the hatch, and Zax froze not knowing whether to flee or reach for the blade in his boot. The Flight Boss did not suffer any hesitation. He pounced and tackled the figure to the ground. A moment later he stood up with what appeared to be a tiny civilian gripped in a vicious, suffocating headlock. The body was so small its legs flailed wildly at least half a meter above the deck. The Boss shifted his position and Zax got a good look at the threat.

"Nolly!"

CHAPTER SEVENTEEN

It was delicious, sir.

"Sir—I know him! Don't hurt him! Stop! Please stop!"

Zax was on the verge of striking the Boss when the man finally reacted to his pleas. Nolly sank to the floor and sobbed between gasps for air. The Omega looked back and forth between the civilian and Zax a couple of times before retreating a few steps to stand with his arms crossed and a bemused expression.

Nolly scampered away as Zax approached but stopped when he felt a gentle hand on his back. Zax knelt and stroked the boy's head for a few mins until his tears had almost entirely subsided. Nolly finally looked up and Zax gave him a warm smile.

"I'm sorry you got hurt, Nolly, but you scared us. We didn't know it was you. What are you doing here? Why didn't you go back to your quarters along with everyone else?"

Nolly opened his mouth to speak, but another spasm of coughs triggered another bout of tears. Zax rubbed the boy's back until the crying was gone again. Nolly drew a couple of final large breaths to cement his calm and then finally spoke.

"I'm s-s-s-s-sorry, s-s-s-s-s-sir, but I didn't see it was you and just wanted to g-g-g-get away."

"Take another minute to breathe, Nolly. It's OK. You're safe. No one is going to hurt you again."

The Flight Boss cleared his throat and started to tap his foot impatiently. Zax couldn't care less. The man *must* have realized he had a child in that chokehold. What would possess someone to continue to harm an innocent kid like that—regardless of their current circumstances?

"It's OK, sir," Nolly whispered. "I'm better now. Thank you."

He sat up and Zax took it as the cue to rise and give the boy some space. A min later Nolly started his story.

"I listened to Imair's advice, sir, and took the apple you gave me to my favorite hiding spot. I come here sometimes if I need to get away from everyone for a little while. It was delicious, sir. Thank you so very much. My mouth felt amazing after eating it, so I decided to close my eyes and enjoy the feeling for just a few mins.

"I must have fallen asleep because when I opened my eyes and started walking around, I realized I was all by myself. It was spooky. I heard a group of people talking in the distance, but when I peeked around a corner I saw it was a big group of angry-looking civilians who all had blasters. I got scared and turned back to try a different route, but then I heard more voices approaching so I came back in here to let them pass. It was a group of three Crew—one Marine with white hair and two cadets."

Zax glanced at the Boss who raised an eyebrow. Nolly continued.

"The Marine had a blaster out which made me scared all over again, so I decided to just stay here and hide in my spot. I was trying to go back to sleep again when I heard the hatch open and you two walked in. I was afraid you were looking for me and would tear the compartment apart, so I made a break for it. You know what happened next."

Nolly turned in the Boss's direction and gave him a look that was equal parts fear and anger. Zax tried to get the boy to focus back on him.

"Nolly—the last group you saw, the one with the Marine with the white hair. Which way were they going?"

The boy paused for a moment to think, and then pointed in the same direction that Zax and the Boss were already headed. Zax sighed with relief and addressed the Boss.

"That's great news, sir, at least we know now that we're on their trail. We should get moving again."

Zax turned back to the boy.

"Nolly—I want you to get back into your hiding space, and I want you to wait—"

"Belay that command, cadet. He's coming with us."

Zax looked at the Boss quizzically. The man walked towards the hatch as he continued.

"He's seen me down here, and I won't risk having him run off to give anyone that intel. He's clearly your pet so you better keep him in line. If he gets in the way once..."

The Omega's words hung in the air and their menace filled Zax with dread. Nolly was so overjoyed at the realization he would no longer be alone that he missed the Boss's threat entirely.

The three of them left the compartment and started down the passageway. They eventually came to a ladder that would bring them up to the same level as Waste Systems Control. Zax started up and then motioned for Nolly to follow. The boy stepped backwards instead.

"No..."

"What?" The Boss went instantly apoplectic. "Get on that ladder, boy!"

The officer's harsh tone took whatever trepidation the young civilian was feeling and increased it to the point that he once again burst into tears. Zax ignored the officer's exasperation, jumped off the ladder, and took a knee to get his face down to the boy's eye level.

"What's going on, Nolly? We need to go up that ladder now, OK? That's where we're going."

The boy slowly shook his head for a while and then finally looked up at Zax. He choked out an explanation through the tears.

"Up there—that's where I saw them. The big angry group with all the blasters."

Zax sighed in relief. Nolly wasn't causing trouble, he was actually helping them out. Zax looked over at the Boss for affirmation of the boy's usefulness, but the man's expression offered nothing. Zax stood and patted the boy on the shoulder.

"That's awesome, Nolly, really awesome. Thank you for helping us avoid that big angry group. We're not going to make you go up right now. We'll take a different path. Let's go."

It was a less direct routing, but Zax led them through a series of passageways and then up a different ladder. Zax eventually motioned for them to halt and gestured for the Boss to approach.

"Sir," he whispered, "that hatch at the end of the passageway is Waste Systems Control."

"OK, cadet, good work. I'll hang back with the boy. I want you to recon and make sure your supervisors are still alone."

The Boss stepped back and put a hand on Nolly's shoulder to keep him in place. The boy visibly recoiled from the man's touch but managed to stay calm. Zax stalked down the passage until he was right up against the hatch.

He barely made out voices, but they were definitely still in there. Zax heard Salmea and Westerick during his initial min of eavesdropping and was about to motion for the Boss and Nolly to join him when a third, more muffled voice joined the conversation. Zax held his breath and listened more intently in an attempt to identify the speaker, but the person was either too far away from the hatch or talking more quietly than the Waste Systems officers.

Zax reached for the hatch and opened it a seemingly imperceptible crack. Before he could do anything more, the hatch exploded open and Zax was flung backwards only to be immediately lifted off the deck by a hand gripped around his throat. He stared down the barrel of a blaster and recognized Sergeant's Bailee red face glaring at him from the other end. After a tense moment, the man released his hold on Zax and grimaced as he switched the blaster back to his uninjured arm.

"It's about time. What took you so long to get here?"

CHAPTER EIGHTEEN

You can thank Captain Clueless over there.

Zax followed the Boss into the compartment and fought back the overwhelming urge to give Kalare a hug when he spotted her. Aleron sat in a corner of the compartment and sported a fresh black eye. Major Westerick and Lieutenant Salmea stood at the hatch to Westerick's office, and Westerick appeared nervous as the Flight Boss entered his domain. Salmea leaned against the bulkhead, indifferent as always to everything going on around her.

Once the perfunctory greetings and introductions were over, the Boss took Sergeant Bailee into Westerick's office along with the Waste Systems officers. Zax assumed it was a strategy meeting for the big minds. And Westerick and Salmea.

Zax sat down for the first time since they had been marched out of Engineering Control by the burly civilian. It had only been a few hours, but it felt like a lifetime. Nolly sat next to him and when the boy yawned Zax suggested he close his eyes and rest. Nolly took this as an invitation to lay his head in Zax's lap and was gently snoring within secs.

Kalare approached and grinned as she took in the scene. She sat next to Zax on the side opposite where Nolly was sprawled. Zax spoke quietly to avoid waking the boy.

"What happened to you guys? You were supposed to wait for me and the Boss to return."

"Tell me about it. You can thank Captain Clueless over there. We—"

"I can hear you two perfectly well, you know!"

Aleron sounded more whiny than he likely intended and Zax stifled a giggle. Kalare sighed dramatically but did so with a sly grin.

"I really couldn't care less about what you hear or don't hear, *Captain Clueless*. As I was saying, we were waiting for you guys and Sergeant Bailee was in pretty rough shape. I suggested we get out of the tunnels and try to locate a medkit. He must have truly been feeling horrible because he agreed without hesitation. The hatch closest to where you left us opened onto an empty passage, so we went down the tunnel and tried a different one where we saw there were a few nearby compartments.

"You told us we'd would be locked out of the tunnels if we let a hatch close behind us, so we left Aleron at the access port and told him to keep it held open while we searched. Not sixty secs later Aleron screams like he's being murdered. We run back and he's jumping up and down, blabbering about a giant rat running out of the tunnel. Of course, he'd managed to let the hatch close behind him. We pounded on it for a while hoping to catch your attention when you passed by, but eventually gave up."

Zax whacked his forehead with the heel of his palm. He and the Boss had actually listened to them pounding from the other side of that hatch. Kalare continued.

"We were rightfully pissed about getting locked out, but the sergeant went a little overboard and slugged Aleron in the face."

Aleron brooded silently and missed how Kalare looked over at him with a healthy degree of sympathy. Zax was taken aback by any show of compassion for the bully and was about to challenge Kalare about it when her expression shifted and she turned back to him.

"What happened with you and the Boss? Who's this kid?"

Zax gave a recap of his journey from the point when they had returned to the meeting spot and found everyone was gone. He described his relationship with Nolly and how they came across the boy. He told her about what happened when Nolly refused to go up the ladder. Kalare raised her eyebrows at the realization there was a group of hostile civilians nearby.

"One more thing I almost forgot. The Boss awarded me bonus credits at one point. Can you believe him? We're in the middle of all this craziness, and he's awarding credits? To me, of all people!"

Kalare had smiled attentively throughout Zax's retelling, but at this point she leaned in and positively beamed.

"Credits! That's awesome, Zax! Do you know what this means? He's warming back up to you. Remember all those credits he gave you when we patched the breach in the panorama last year—can you imagine how many you could earn for rescuing him from civilians? You can get right back to the top of the Leaderboard and join me in the Flight Academy!"

Zax was shocked to hear Kalare draw the same conclusion he had reached earlier. He gave her the same rationale which had led him to immediately dismiss it.

"Are you nuts? I publicly accused one of the Omegas of murder and the Boss has to know I was really talking about him. There's no way in hell he would ever award me anywhere near enough credits to make a difference in my ranking! Besides, he probably blames me for all of this mess in the first place given how I exposed the video of that human fighter."

"Don't be silly, Zax. When all this blows over, he's not going to have any choice. You're right—he's not going to *want* to support you given the history between you two, but there's no way he'd be able to let the cadet who rescued him go away empty-handed. Working with him, I've come to learn how much the Boss considers potential Crew perceptions when making decisions. I'm pretty sure he didn't immediately Cull you back then because he didn't want to give your accusations any more weight in the Crew's eyes. Rewarding you now will make people forget about those allegations altogether. Most people prefer simple narrative and you'll be transformed in their eyes from the cadet who accused an Omega of murder to the cadet who saved the Boss. You're easily looking at five-figures worth of bonus credits!"

Zax disregarded the possibility of significant rewards earlier, but if Kalare was reaching the same conclusion then perhaps there was some validity to the notion. He clearly had achieved far beyond what would be expected of a typical cadet through all of this ordeal. Kalare might be right in thinking his actions would merit acknowledgement with serious credits once this uprising by the civilians was over—even if it meant the Boss had to get past his distaste for rewarding Zax of all people.

What about Zax's distaste for the Boss? Even if Kalare was convinced the man was innocent, Zax still held him accountable for Mikedo's death. Working in Waste Systems, however, was doing nothing to prove Zax's suspicions and make the Omega pay. Maybe if Zax could put aside his feelings and get himself closer to the Boss again, he'd be able to learn what he needed to see the man punished.

Zax's deliberations were interrupted by the opening of the hatch to Westerick's office. Bailee walked out and looked at Zax and Kalare.

"Come in here. The Boss wants you to hear this firsthand."

Aleron stood to join them, but the Marine shook his head.

"Not you. Someone needs to stay here and keep an eye on the civilian."

Aleron was indignant for a moment, but then his face brightened.

"That means I should get the blaster then, right?"

The sergeant turned back and grinned at the cadet. Zax recognized the look as a dangerous signal, but Aleron once again lived up to the "Captain Clueless" nickname as he held out his hand for the weapon.

"You're saying you need my weapon to stand watch over an eight-year-old boy. Who's asleep. I'm sorry, cadet, but I realize now that I must have knocked something loose in your head when I hit you earlier. Maybe you need another punch to settle things back into place."

The Marine smiled coldly at Aleron and the cadet's face went as red as his shirt. Zax extricated himself from beneath Nolly without waking the boy and followed Kalare and the sergeant into the compartment. The Boss looked up as they entered.

"Here's the plan—"

CHAPTER NINETEEN

We can pretend all of that silliness
never happened.

"A Marine garrison is located in the next section, and there will be a significant force there to protect the armory. We need to reach them. I'm certain the civilians are actively targeting me, and it's critical for the survival of the Ship that I get more protection as soon as feasibly possible. Even though Salmea and Westerick can access their Plugs, the civilians have blocked all communication. We can't call the Marines to us, so we have no choice but to make our way to them."

The Boss looked at each of them for a few beats before he nodded to acknowledge Kalare's raised hand.

"Sir—why do you feel the civilians are targeting you? If they wanted you that badly, why would their leader back in Engineering have let you out of his sight?"

"That's a great question, Kalare, but, unfortunately, the answer is on a need-to-know basis. Let me assure you the civilians' strategic situation has changed, and I'm confident they now see me as critical to their plans to secure control of the Ship."

The Boss let the idea of civilian control sink in for a moment before he continued.

"With Zax's help it should be easy to get most of the way to our destination using the maintenance tunnels, but we can't get all the way there. For security purposes, the Marines blocked the tunnels that approach their garrison so the last portion of our journey must be through the main passageways. I'm guessing the civilians will be as far from the Marines as they can possibly be. We aren't likely to run into any hostiles, but you never know. Keeping me safe is the most important thing any of you are likely to do in your lifetime. Do it well, and I promise your efforts will be recognized.

"I need some time alone before we leave, so give me the room. Zax—hang back, please."

Zax had keyed in on the Boss's mention of being "recognized," and Kalare must have as well because she gave him an encouraging thumbs up as she walked past to exit the compartment along with the others. Once the hatch was closed and they were alone, the Boss smiled at Zax for a few long, uncomfortable moments before speaking.

"You must be able to appreciate the strange predicament I find myself in here, Zax. I gave you an amazing opportunity a year ago. You were on the verge of not only becoming a pilot but also gaining me as your mentor. You took that opportunity and threw it away in nearly the most disastrous way possible."

Zax shuffled his feet. It had been easy to nurse his hatred and distrust of the man over the past year when the Boss was a never-seen figure who existed only in Kalare's stories. It was entirely different to share a compartment with the Omega while the man smiled and spoke with him like a peer rather than a despised underling. Zax was being charmed by the man and what made it painfully uncomfortable was how he found himself liking it. Kalare had suggested that redemption was possible and against his better instincts Zax wanted to grasp for it. The Boss leaned forward and spoke again.

"These are extreme circumstances we find ourselves in, and there's no way I can ignore how admirably well you've performed so far. I want to encourage you to reconsider whatever grudges you've held against me during your year here in Waste Systems. Having spent all of fifteen mins with your supervisors, I think I can appreciate what that time has been like for you."

The Boss paused and grinned, and Zax couldn't help but join in as well.

"So here's the deal, Zax. I mentioned to the group how crucial it is I stay out of the hands of the civilians. I can't stress this enough. If we get out of this mess and you play the critical role I need you to, then you're going to find yourself right back at the top of the Leaderboard with me as your mentor just like you were a year ago. We can pretend all of that silliness never happened. What do you think?"

The Boss's grin had disappeared and been replaced with a look of intense focus. Zax was conflicted. Hearing the Boss refer to everything around Mikedo's death, however obliquely, as being silly made him angry. Leaving the hell of Waste Systems and getting his career back on track for the Flight Academy, however, was a powerful inducement. Nothing was being served by wasting his life maintaining the Ship's sewers. He could never do anything to rewrite the story of Mikedo's sacrifice from down here. If he actually spent time close to the Boss, then maybe he would discover the evidence that would finally allow him to prove beyond a doubt the man had killed her. He would always despise who he was making the deal with, but Zax was smart enough to realize it was the right deal. He didn't trust himself to speak so he just nodded in agreement. The Boss smiled.

"Good decision, Zax. Please go join the others. I'll be out in a moment."

Zax exited the compartment. Kalare approached him immediately and whispered excitedly.

"What was that about?"

"Exactly what you were thinking. If I help keep him away from the civilians, he's going to give me enough credits to put me back on top of the Leaderboard. I could get into the Pilot Academy. And he's going to be my mentor."

"Holy crap, Zax! That's amazing! Are you excited?"

Zax was excited but remained conflicted. The nuances of the situation were impossible to convey with quick whispers, so he only nodded in reply. He would share all of this thinking with Kalare at some point down the road. Or maybe he wouldn't.

She smiled and at that moment Bailee approached and addressed Zax.

"Cadet—wake up your civilian, please. We need to talk about what's going to happen next, and I need him to hear it."

Zax went to Nolly and roused the boy. He had fallen asleep instantly, but waking him up proved a far more onerous chore. Zax prodded the child repeatedly and finally spoke to him harshly before he opened his eyes. Zax helped Nolly to his feet, and once the Marine saw the boy was alert, Bailee started to speak.

"We're making our way to a nearby Marine garrison. We'll keep the following formation. Zax is going to be on point, followed by the civilian and

Kalare. Then it is going to be me and the Boss. Aleron, then Lieutenant Salmea, and finally Major Westerick will bring up the rear. We still only have the one blaster, and I'm going to hold on to it. Remember—our goal above all else is to prevent the Boss from getting captured by the civilians. Is that all clear?"

The Marine sternly looked each person in the eye, and everyone except Nolly silently nodded. Nolly was so intimidated by the man's glare that he buried his face in Zax's side. The Flight Boss came out of Westerick's office and looked around the compartment.

"Move out."

CHAPTER TWENTY

We can't let you have all the fun today.

They started down the hallway in the formation Bailee specified. Their initial destination was an access port one hundred meters away which would get them back into the maintenance network. They had covered a quarter of the distance when they heard running footsteps behind them. It sounded like a single person making absolutely no attempt at stealth.

Everyone looked to Bailee for instruction, and he gestured for them to move tight against the bulkhead. He positioned himself at the corner where the running person would soon emerge and clasped his blaster at the ready. Zax held his breath as the footsteps grew closer and closer until a woman appeared.

"Imair!"

Nolly called out, broke loose from Zax's grasp, and dashed towards the woman. Imair initially kept running towards the boy, but then must have noticed Bailee and his blaster out of the corner of her eye. She skidded to a halt with her hands in the air. Nolly closed the gap on his own and threw his arms around the woman in a desperate embrace. The two stood frozen and the Marine tensed his finger on his weapon's trigger. All other eyes looked to Zax for an explanation.

"I know her. Her name's Imair and she works in Waste Systems. She's OK."

The Boss turned to Imair and barked out an interrogation.

"Civilian—what are you doing here? Why aren't you in your quarters with everyone else? What are you running from?"

Imair's eyes went wide with recognition when she saw the Boss. She had no doubt seen him in countless newsvids with zero expectation of ever seeing him in the flesh. She kept her arms up as she turned slowly to him, took a deep breath, and spoke with a tremulous voice.

"My profuse apologies, sir. I've been searching all over the civilian barracks for this boy, and when I finally determined he was absent, I figured he must still be down here. I nominated him for his job in Waste Systems, so I feel responsible for him. I was running because I'm desperate to find him and get us both back to safety as fast as I can."

The Boss sighed loudly.

"Stand down, Sergeant. Frisk her thoroughly, but unless you find anything, it looks like our little traveling party has grown by one civilian. Keep a close eye on her and take care of things if she does *anything* remotely suspicious."

Kalare helped Zax peel Nolly off Imair so the civilian could place her arms against the bulkhead and submit to the Marine's search of her body. He was fairly rough and extremely thorough, but he ultimately was satisfied she had nothing hidden on her person. The Marine went over to speak quietly with the Boss, and Imair approached Zax.

"Hello, sir. Thank you for identifying me. Probably the only thing which prevented that Marine from blasting. Pretty strange running into you down here."

"Pretty strange day all around, Imair. Don't worry—you and Nolly are going to be safe. We're on our way to join up with some Marines and we'll be able to get most of the way there by way of the maintenance tunnels. Civilians can't get in there so we shouldn't run into any of the rebels."

"Thank you, sir. I'd rather be back in the barracks away from all of this violence, but I imagine being with Marines who are guarding the Flight Boss is probably a decent second option."

"Everyone—time to move out again."

Imair grabbed Nolly's hand in response to the sergeant's command and fell into formation behind

Zax and Kalare. The Marine followed close behind with his blaster, even more alert than he had been a few mins earlier if such a thing was possible.

They reached the tunnels without further incident and Westerick went wide-eyed as he looked around. The man must have never been inside the maintenance network before. How someone could have worked in Waste Systems for so long and never bothered to visit the tunnels seemed crazy but in line with Zax's experience of the man.

They navigated roughly a thousand meters of tunnels and ladders until they reached the security bulkhead which blocked the approach to the Marine garrison. It hadn't appeared on the schematics Zax studied, and its hatch did not respond to his security clearance. It was also plastered with explicit warnings about what fate would befall anyone who attempted to breach it. They backtracked to the last access port they had seen and gathered around to hear what the Boss wanted next.

"We're close, but there's still a good chunk of passageway between us and the Marines. With this big of a group, I think it's important for us to know exactly what we're walking into before we head out. I'm going to have someone scout ahead and report back."

Zax started towards the hatch under the assumption he was the best candidate given his ability to navigate. The Boss called after him.

"Actually, Zax, I'm going to send Kalare. Brief her on the layout of the passageways so she can find her way to the edge of the garrison and back."

"But sir, wouldn't it make more sense for me to go? If anything happens, I'll be better suited to improvise and figure out an alternate path if needed."

"I understand, cadet, but your ability to get in and out of the maintenance network is too valuable to risk on this mission. You are second only to Bailee in importance when it comes to keeping me out of the hands of the hostiles, so you're going to stick close. *Agreed*?"

The Boss's tone invited no further discussion, and the question at the end of his statement was clearly rhetorical. Zax walked slowly towards the hatch with Kalare and discussed the route she should take. After she repeated it back to him twice, they paused and looked awkwardly at each other until Kalare broke the silence.

"Thanks, Zax. We can't let you have all the fun today."

Kalare smiled, but her apprehension about heading into the unknown by herself was evident. They arranged two different codes for her to bang out on the hatch when she returned. One meant "all clear" and they should let her in while the other signaled she was under duress and had been forced to lead civilians back to the hatch. Zax couldn't imagine leaving Kalare to her fate in the second scenario and desperately hoped his ability to do so wouldn't be tested.

Once Kalare left they secured the hatch and everyone settled down to rest. Well, everyone except Nolly. He overflowed with energy after the long nap he had taken earlier. Imair absorbed his exuberance with a warm smile. She cheerfully engaged with every random story the boy threw at her and even played along with a game he devised which involved climbing up the first few rungs of a nearby ladder to see how far he could reach with a subsequent jump.

The Crew watched the civilian woman and boy interact with varying degrees of interest and tolerance. In any other circumstance, Zax would have appreciated watching Nolly's carefree abandon, but he was overcome with worry about Kalare and grateful Imair had shown up to wrangle the boy. Westerick and Salmea glanced at the young civilian and grinned occasionally at his frolicking, but generally chatted among themselves. Aleron had nothing to occupy him except the boy's antics, and the cadet's pouting seemed to intensify the more Imair and Nolly giggled among themselves. The Boss sat with his eyes closed and breathed slowly. If it was anyone else, Zax would have guessed they were sound asleep, but he knew the Boss was capable of springing into action in a heartbeat. Sergeant Bailee never took his eyes off Imair and kept his trigger finger ready the entire time.

Zax had been sitting with his eyes closed when he heard a bang on the hatch. He bolted upright and held his breath. After recognizing the all clear code, he exhaled in gratitude. He knew that Kalare was probably even more capable than he was in dangerous and tricky situations, but he held himself responsible for protecting his friend nonetheless. He opened the hatch to let Kalare in and then secured it behind her. Bailee and the Boss arrived immediately, though the Marine continued to watch Imair as he listened to Kalare.

"I was able to get almost all of the way there, but near the end I saw two civilians with blasters. They seemed bored and were chatting with each other, but they are clearly not just there randomly."

The Boss grilled Kalare for more details about the exact location of the civilians and then looked at the sergeant with a raised eyebrow. The Marine nodded in response, and the Omega called everyone else to gather round.

"We've only got two hostiles between us and the Marine garrison, so we're going to make it. Here's what I want us to do. We'll hold our formation as we approach just in case they end up being on the move or we encounter anyone else. Once we are around the corner from them, the boy will step into their line of sight and get their attention. Once he does—"

"Excuse me, sir, did you just say that you're going to use an eight-year-old as a diversion?"

Sergeant Bailee bristled at Imair's interruption of the Boss and color flooded his cheeks. The Boss appraised the civilian for a moment with an expression that suggested amusement rather than anger. Nolly had continued to play his climb and jump game on the ladder and was missing out on all of the tension over his role in the mission. The Boss looked straight at Imair and spoke.

"The boy will step into their line of sight and get their attention. From Kalare's description, these folks are bored and not primed to shoot the first thing that moves. Once it's clear they've been distracted by the boy, Sergeant Bailee is going to pop around the corner and dispatch them. Let's move."

Zax watched Imair but the civilian was clearly smart enough to not press her luck. Her desire to protect the boy was admirable, but she had to have recognized how the Boss and Marine were barely tolerating the civilians' presence. Bailee in particular did not need any reason to remove Imair as a potential threat. She gathered the boy and spoke quietly to him for a moment while everyone else made ready to head out.

CHAPTER TWENTY-ONE

I know where one is.

The group exited the tunnels and traversed the main passageways silently. Kalare eventually signaled a halt and gestured that the pair of civilians were around the next corner. Bailee crept to the edge of the passageway and pulled a shiny scrap of broken material out of his pocket. Its surface reflected back what was around the corner, and he confirmed with an OK sign that the civilians were present as expected.

The Boss sidled up to Nolly and got down on one knee to speak softly in the boy's ear. Zax observed how the Omega was pulling out all of the stops to put the boy at ease—including giving the child a hug of all crazy things! The boy looked up at Imair for reassurance, and she hid the worry she surely felt and gave him a double thumbs up.

Nolly shuffled to where Sergeant Bailee continued to monitor the hostiles around the corner. The Marine held up his hand for the boy to stop for a moment and then signaled him forwards. The boy turned the corner and froze. A voice called out immediately from down the passageway and ordered Nolly to remain still. It was likely the easiest command the boy ever followed since he probably had zero ability to move.

In a flash, the Marine leapt around the corner and fired two blaster shots in quick succession. Nolly scampered back into Imair's embrace and wailed into her chest as the sergeant gave the all clear. Zax regretted the need to get the boy involved, but, all things considered, it had been a pretty easy task.

Zax looked around the corner. The Marine stood at the far end of the passage and checked the next junction. He must have moved the two bodies out of the way because the civilians were piled atop one another against the bulkhead. There wasn't any blood visible yet, and Zax hoped for Nolly's sake they could make their way past the corpses before any seeped out from under them. The Marine brushed past Zax and whispered to the Boss. A moment later he rotated a finger in the air and pointed forwards. It was time to move down the passageway, and the formation turned the corner and moved past the dead civilians.

Zax breathed easier with every step which brought them closer to the Marine garrison. It was the right decision to rescue the Boss and Bailee a few hours back, but the non-stop stress of their journey since had worn his nerves raw and he suffered from an acute adrenalin hangover. All forward momentum depended on the waning excitement from the reward the Omega had dangled. Zax was relieved to reach the Marines primarily because it meant the professionals would inherit the task of protecting the Boss.

For the second time that day, the sudden appearance of armed civilians shocked Zax. At least half a dozen materialized, as if by magic, at the end of the passageway. They opened fire immediately and the air filled with the sound of blasters.

In all of the confusion, it sounded like more than one blaster was being discharged at the civilians. Zax knew that was impossible since only Bailee was armed. The Marine charged to the front of their formation and screamed for everyone else to fall back around the corner.

Zax spun and bolted back the way they had come. The Boss and Waste Systems officers, along with Aleron, were already gone. Imair, shielding Nolly with her body, was rounding the corner and Kalare followed a few steps behind.

The group paused once they were out of the line of fire while blasters raged in the passageway behind them. Zax was clueless about what they might do if Bailee was killed. He looked around for the Boss to see if the officer had any orders.

The Omega slumped against the bulkhead a short distance away from everyone else. He grimaced as a blood stain pooled on his shirt. He appeared to be talking to himself, which struck Zax as an extremely odd reaction to getting shot. The Boss noticed Zax's attention and turned away. Just then Bailee charged around the corner and barked out a command.

"Zax—get everyone into the tunnels! I can hold them for a few mins longer and will be right behind you!"

They dashed back to the access port the group had exited a short while earlier. The Boss hobbled but managed to keep up with the rest of them. Zax used his biometrics to open the hatch and stepped aside and directed everyone else to enter.

"Hurry up and get in! I'm going to hold the hatch open for the sergeant, but if anyone other than him comes around that corner, I'm slamming it shut!"

The group piled through the hatch quickly except for the Boss. The Omega was the last to approach and he paused a few extra secs before finally ducking into the tunnel. Zax guessed the man must be in shock from his wound and blood loss.

Zax turned his attention back down the passage just as Sergeant Bailee sprinted around the corner. The Marine stopped for a moment to lay down a barrage of blaster fire behind him, and then made another mad dash towards the hatch. He screamed at Zax.

"They're right behind me! Get that hatch secured as soon as I'm in!"

The Marine dove into the tunnel as the first civilians turned the corner firing wildly. Zax felt the heat from a shot within centimeters of his head as he slammed and secured the hatch. He collapsed against the bulkhead for a moment to catch his breath.

The Marine appeared amazingly unfazed, especially in light of the fact he had been running around all day with a broken collarbone. He jumped immediately to the Boss's aid and gingerly pulled away the man's shirt to check the wound.

"He's got a bad bleeder. We might be able to stop it with pressure, but we could sure use a medkit."

Zax thought for a moment but then shook his head.

"It's almost exclusively civilians in Waste Systems, so we don't keep any medkits around. I can't even guess where we might find one nearby."

Imair stood to speak.

"I know where one is."

CHAPTER TWENTY-TWO

He will be awake in thirty mins.

The Boss propped himself against Sergeant Bailee as they both listened intently as Imair spoke.

"The civilian staff requested a medkit be kept in Waste Systems years ago because so many workers got injured working in the deep caverns. Open wounds and sewage aren't a great combination, and it took too long for the injured to make their way back up for medical care. Major Westerick denied our request, but someone took it upon themselves to steal a kit from a different section. We've managed to appropriate enough supplies to keep it functional ever since."

"Where is it?" The Boss coughed out his question, but there was no blood coming out of his mouth.

"In the sewage treatment cavern."

The Boss turned to Zax. "Can you get us there?"

Zax grimaced but realized they had no choice given the Boss's condition. He nodded as he replied. "Yes, sir."

Zax paused frequently during the group's march back into the depths. He checked on the Boss to be sure the pace he was setting was feasible given the man's injury. The officer's shirt was thoroughly soaked with blood, but he continued to move as fast as Zax was leading them. The Omega had his faults, but Zax could never deny he was tough.

The air became thicker and thicker with the reek of human waste the deeper the group descended. More than once, someone behind Zax gagged on the stench. If folks were having an issue with the odor now, he couldn't wait to see how they handled it once they reached the treatment cavern. The smells there were beyond horrific but even worse were the sights. What he saw with his eyes led him to vomit the one time he had visited.

Eventually, the group reached the bottom of their final ladder. By the looks of the Boss, they had reached their destination just in time. The officer was forced to lean on Sergeant Bailee for support as they walked the final one hundred meters to the cavern. Zax opened the final hatch and stood aside to allow everyone to enter.

When Zax followed the last person through, he couldn't help but gawk at the size of the space even though he had visited previously. There were precious few spaces on board the Ship which were as large in volume as the treatment cavern, with only the Flight Hangar being bigger. Unlike the wide-open space of the hangar, the treatment cavern was jam-packed with the massive containers which were the heart of the sewage system.

Everything on board the Ship needed to be reused and recycled for maximum effectiveness and the waste output of ten million humans was no exception. The fifty-meter-tall vessels converted all of the feces and urine into a relatively benign sludge which was used to fertilize crops. Each was constructed of stainless steel. Legend held they had gleamed like mirrors generations ago, but that was hard to imagine given their current appearance. Innumerable accidental overflows during the most recent decades had caked the outsides of each egg-shaped container with a thick, oozing layer of biological sludge. The gasses associated with this ancient accumulation occasionally shifted from horrific to truly dangerous and required the use of secondary breathers until the methane concentrations abated.

As treacherous as the air sometimes became, it didn't compare to the other dangers which lurked throughout the cavern. All of the machinery, in addition to being festooned with human waste, was designed such that it lacked almost all of the safety features found in other systems Zax had encountered around the Ship. One careless mistake on the part of the sewage treatment workers could easily lead to injuries, amputations, or worse.

Zax heard a retching noise and looked over just in time to watch Major Westerick bend over and puke between his feet. Salmea immediately followed his lead. Imair caught Zax's eye and they shared a sly smile at the sight of the two officers getting a taste of what life in Waste Systems was like for everyone other than them.

The civilian woman turned and walked quickly away from the group. Sergeant Bailee was clearly agitated about her sudden and unannounced movement, but he held his tongue and followed from a few paces behind. The Marine was so focused on Imair that he missed seeing the Boss collapse to the deck. Aleron and Kalare jumped to the Omega's aid in his place.

Imair moved to the far side of the cavern and pushed aside a workstation. Its back must have been hollowed out because she pulled a Crew medkit out from behind it. She wheeled the kit back and set it up next to the Boss. Imair turned and addressed Bailee who had remained a couple paces behind the civilian throughout.

"Sergeant—you're doing an amazing job considering you've got a banged up arm, but with your permission I think it would be better if I treated the officer."

The Marine nodded his assent, but there remained an unspoken threat in the posture he adopted.

Before Imair got started, she took off her shirt and placed it under the Boss's head balled up as a pillow. It struck Zax as an unnecessarily kind gesture considering the man appeared to finally be unconscious. She next started to remove the Boss's shirt. She had undone the fasteners and was about to pull his arms out of the sleeves when Sergeant Bailee interrupted.

"No—leave the shirt on. Just pull it up on the side of the wound."

Imair gave the Marine a look of confusion but, after a moment, shook her head and followed the man's instructions. She pulled the shirt up, and Zax got a clear look at the damage. The energy bolt from the civilian blaster had hit the Omega in the side. The wound oozed blood and was clearly life-threatening, but the Boss was lucky it hadn't hit a few centimeters more towards the center of his body where it would have shredded organs.

The civilian popped the latch on the medkit and it butterflied open. A vidscreen dominated the top portion of its left half, and a series of compartments and ports of varying sizes were distributed throughout the remainder. She removed a small disc and fastened it to the Boss's temple and then a slightly larger one which she applied to his chest above the heart. The monitor came to life and displayed the Omega's vital signs. Zax had been given introductory training on the use of a medkit and knew enough to recognize how the flashing yellow symbols showed the man to be in serious condition, albeit with a good chance of survival.

Imair next extracted a long wand from the kit. She slowly waved it over the site of the wound. As she did so, a 3D rendering appeared on the screen and detailed the extent of the damage. Once again, the display was dominated by the yellow symbols which showed the man's condition to be serious, but not yet deadly. A red number flashed a countdown until the medkit would be ready to proceed.

While the medkit counted down the time, Imair prepped the Boss for treatment. She opened a compartment and removed a small, circular device with a transparent hose attached. She plugged the hose into one of the ports on the medkit and then attached the other end to the Boss's forearm between his wrist and elbow. The next device Imair grabbed was much larger and rectangular shaped. It also had a transparent hose which the civilian plugged into yet another port before she placed the square end over the Omega's wound. Suction formed a vacuum around the wound and Zax could see the indent the device caused where it pressed into the man's body.

The countdown flashed a green 00:00:00, and Imair double-checked the placement of each device and which port they were plugged into. She looked up at Bailee for his approval and the Marine nodded. She pressed a flashing green button and then leaned back to watch.

The first thing Zax saw was bright green liquid ooze out of the medkit and down the tube into the circular device attached to the Boss's arm. He recognized the plasma which would replace the man's blood loss. It was filled with artificial red blood cells which would help oxygenate the officer. These were programmed to slowly die off and be flushed out of his system over the next hundred days as the man's body recovered and replaced them with the real thing.

Shortly after the plasma flowed into the Boss's arm, a dark blue liquid flowed out of the larger tube into the square device which covered the wound. Zax remembered from his training how this liquid had numerous properties. First, it was a broad spectrum antibiotic which would cleanse the wound, a critical activity given their current surroundings. Second, the liquid was filled with nanobots which would swarm through the wound and repair any and all damage at the cellular level. Finally, it contained a material which would form a matrix to close the wound and protect it during the healing process. This matrix would dissolve over days and weeks as the body regenerated tissue around it until eventually the patient would look down and see nothing but new, smooth skin.

After a few mins of working its magic, the medkit sounded a notification to signal completion. Imair removed the various devices and returned them to their compartments where they would be automatically cleaned and sterilized for the next patient. She looked up at the Marine and spoke.

"He'll be awake in thirty mins. After that, he'll need to rest for another forty-five to allow the protective matrix to complete formation. How about I take a quick look at that arm, Sergeant?"

The Marine hesitated for a moment but then nodded and sat down next to the medkit. Imair removed the diagnostic wand once more and waved it over Bailee's shoulder. The screen revealed the man's collarbone had not been broken but instead shattered. His ability to move his arm, much less tolerate the intense activity he had participated in over the past few hours was truly inhuman. Imair gave a low whistle of appreciation as she surveyed the damage.

"Well, there's your problem right there, Sergeant. It looks like your arm is about to fall off. Let's get a patch on you, and the medkit can take a genetic sample and brew up the right binding agent to repair that bone."

The Marine shook his head. "I can't afford to have my arm numbed right now while the binder sets. It will keep." He stood up to indicate there would be no further discussion of the matter. "Zax—search all the workstations and storage lockers to see if you can find any food. I'm hoping maybe one of the workers kept something around in case they ever got hungry in these beautiful surroundings. Unless, of course, the female civilian already knows where any other supplies might be stashed away like the medkit was."

CHAPTER TWENTY-THREE

Why are you nice to me?

Imair assured Bailee she wasn't aware of any hidden food. There would usually be serious trouble if something like a stolen medkit was discovered in a civilian area, but Zax had to hope the Omegas would look the other way this time. Revealing the civilians' secret was a brave and selfless act, and Zax hoped Imair would get rewarded somehow when all of this was over. If she said she didn't know where any food was located, then Zax believed her.

Zax looked over at the young civilian. The boy was siting a few meters away and had watched wide-eyed from behind Kalare and Aleron as Imair used the medkit to fix up the Boss and check out Bailee.

"Hey, Nolly—do you want to help me tear apart all of the workstations and storage lockers over there to see if we can find something to eat?"

A huge grin spread across the boy's face as he popped to his feet. He had stopped clinging to Zax in favor of Imair once she appeared, but he seemed thrilled by the prospect of spending time with his favorite member of the Crew. Particularly if it involved an adventure which sounded both illicit and destructive. He sprinted off towards the far end of the cavern.

Aleron stood as Nolly ran off and called out to Zax. "You two check out the far side over there and I'll search the storage areas on this side."

It seemed curious that Aleron was trying to be helpful all of a sudden. He must be hoping to restore some goodwill with Bailee if he could be the one to discover food. Zax turned and jogged to catch up with Nolly. The boy had stopped running but bounced on his toes with anticipation. Zax had just about caught up to the young civilian when he saw that Kalare was similarly jogging after Aleron. Kalare wanting to be alone with Captain Clueless was even more strange than Aleron being useful and filled Zax with such consternation that he slowed to a halt to ponder the matter.

"Excuse me, sir. Why are you nice to me?"

Nolly's question took Zax by surprise and yanked his attention away from concerns about Kalare. He didn't have an answer so instead responded with a question of his own. "Why wouldn't I be?"

"Well, no one else from the Crew is ever nice to me. The man who was bleeding forced me to go out into that passageway all by myself. The other man with the white hair scared me by shooting his blaster right behind me. None of the other Crew we're with have ever said anything to me at all."

"I can't speak for the officer or the Marine, but I'll say that most of the other Crew never have an opportunity to work with civilians, so they might not be very comfortable around you. I've been working in Waste Systems for a year now, and you've always been super nice and helpful to me. It would be pretty bad of me to not return the favor, right?"

"Thank you, sir. I hope if I get to be in the Crew when I get older that I still get to work with civilians and don't forget about being nice to them."

The shock caused by Nolly's statement nearly made Zax fall flat on his face. How could the boy think he could ever become a member of the Crew? What did the civilians teach their children? Zax had been taught for as long as he could remember how the original Crew were chosen due to being perfectly suited for the mission of commanding the Ship. Hundreds of generations worth of artificial breeding since then had focused on genetic optimization to reinforce their critical traits. Crew weren't born through the genetic crapshoot of procreation and then influenced by whatever might happen while gestating within a woman's belly. They were designed by the well-honed algorithms of the Genetics AI and then nurtured through birth within the ideal conditions of the Ship's artificial wombs.

Civilians, by contrast, were allowed to breed however they saw fit once a female was given permission to have children. Whatever random attraction happened to bring together a man and a woman created offspring which were equally random. They supported the Ship in lower value roles like those in Waste Systems, but it was absurd to think civilians were capable of much more.

Zax debated whether he should be the one to help Nolly understand the proper distinction between Crew and civilian and what his future would hold, but he decided that was better left to whatever crazy system the civilians used for educating their offspring. Thankfully, the discussion was dropped altogether when the boy sprinted ahead and started yanking drawers out of workstations and dumping their contents onto the deck with wild abandon. Zax smiled at the boy's excitement and set out on his own path of destruction.

The first few drawers Zax checked held nothing interesting, only random collections of paper and the various detritus which collects as someone does their job through the years. Zax couldn't imagine working all day long in a place which looked so repulsive and smelled so vile, but obviously there were dozens of civilians who had no choice but to do so. The drawers of their workstations looked like their jobs were just as boring and routine as Zax's.

"Check this out, sir!"

Zax walked over to where Nolly was holding a Crew slate he had found. The device would only work when activated by the biometrics of the owner, so Zax knew it was futile for a civilian to have stolen one. Away from its owner it was about as useful as a rock. There was no sense in risking additional trouble for the workers in this compartment beyond what they already faced because of the medkit, so Zax told Nolly to return the slate to the drawer where he found it and get back to searching.

They checked all of the workstation drawers without success, and then Zax and Nolly moved on to the storage lockers. After a few mins of rooting around Nolly called out excitedly.

"I've found some food, sir. It's amazing!"

Zax's stomach grumbled at the prospect of sustenance, and he walked to where Nolly stood in front of a locker. The boy pointed inside and Zax followed his gaze to a box of nutripellets.

"It's nutripellets, sir, I LOVE nutripellets! They're so amazingly tasty and filling compared to what we usually get in the mess hall. I know Imair is going to be super excited too. Can I be the one to tell her, please? Please?"

The only thing which would have been worse in Zax's opinion than finding no food was finding nutripellets. The disgusting, chewy nuggets had sustained Zax for days at a time whenever he needed to keep his belly empty for repeated FTL jumps, but he had long fantasized about never eating another once he was Plugged In. Of course, that hadn't worked out as expected. Zax sighed but took small solace in the amount of delight Nolly expressed. Zax signaled for the boy to grab the box and run off to Imair so he could announce their big find.

After Zax checked the last few lockers to no avail, he returned to where the group had spread out to wait. The others among the Crew must have felt the same antipathy for the nutripellets because the box, along with a pile of empty wrappers, sat between Nolly and Imair. Nolly had such a look of pure contentment on his face that Zax could not help but grin out of appreciation for the boy's innocence.

Zax's smile melted away when he noticed that Kalare was back sitting next to Aleron again. Even worse was discovering that they were engaged in an animated conversation which involved both excessive smiling and frequent laughter. Zax wanted to march over and investigate what was behind this disturbing turn of events, but movement in his peripheral vision drew his attention to the Boss. The Omega was unsteadily trying to stand as he barked a question.

"Why is everyone just sitting around?"

CHAPTER TWENTY-FOUR

Permission to speak freely, sir?

Imair bolted up to assist the Boss. "Sir—with all due respect you really need to rest for another forty-five mins. If the protective matrix doesn't have a chance to completely gel, you're just going to start bleeding all over again."

The civilian tried to guide the officer towards a nearby chair, but he brushed her aside. She stood back only to pounce once more when he stumbled and nearly toppled to the ground. He accepted her assistance the second time it was offered and wobbled his way to the chair.

"Damn sedatives—they get me every time. If anything else happens and you need to use that thing on me again, make sure you instruct it to skip the anesthetic."

"Yes, sir."

The Boss looked at Sergeant Bailee who had stood when the Omega stirred but had remained a few meters away and kept a close eye on Imair's interactions with him. "Sergeant—sitrep?"

"Situation is exactly what you see, sir. The medkit patched you up and we've been waiting for you to wake. Unless the boy has managed to eat them all, there are nutripellets if you're hungry enough to eat those. Otherwise, we've got another forty-three mins until the medkit says you're cleared for action."

The Boss made a sour face at the suggestion he eat a nutripellet. "How's your arm, Sergeant? Did you get that patched up while you were waiting on me?"

Imair started to open her mouth, but the Marine shot her a glance and she changed her mind. He replied to the Boss.

"I'm fine, sir. Thank you for asking. What's the plan once you're mobile, sir?"

"I'm thinking that through, Sergeant. Give me a few more mins to gather my thoughts, and then I'll be looking for your input."

Imair went to sit down, but stopped and addressed the Boss instead.

"Sir—I'm assuming this is your first chance to visit Waste Systems. I'm curious to hear your thoughts about it."

The Omega stared at the civilian for a long moment. Zax assumed the man would react with displeasure about the woman trying to start a conversation with him, but he must have been still suffering from the aftereffects of the sedative because he eventually smiled instead.

"It sounds like there might be an ulterior motive behind that question. Is there something you would like to say to me?"

"Permission to speak freely, sir?"

"By all means. I suppose I can entertain a frank conversation in exchange for you telling us about the medkit."

Imair paused for a moment and appeared to gather her thoughts.

"Sir, please take a good, long look around you. Accompany it with a deep breath. When we walked into this cavern, the two officers over there who are responsible for it immediately puked on their shoes. A group of civilians risked the severe punishment involved with stealing that medkit because this work area is so dangerous and toxic they felt they were left with no choice. Too many of their coworkers had died needlessly. Don't you think an awful lot about this cavern would be different if it was Crew who spent their lives working here instead of civilians?"

It took all of his focus for Zax to prevent his mouth from dropping open in shock. Imair was outright challenging the second highest ranking officer on the Ship about her perceived slights around civilian working conditions. Sergeant Bailee tensed substantially, and the Marine's finger tapped next to the trigger of his blaster. Kalare wore an expression which signaled she was struggling to stifle an inappropriate laughing fit. Aleron and the Waste System's officers had pointedly turned away and were pretending to ignore the conversation. Nolly smacked his lips in blissful ignorance as he chomped on yet another nutripellet. The Boss's eyes narrowed as Imair's words sunk in.

"Those are some tough observations, but I appreciate hearing that feedback from you. The Omegas are always thinking about how we can make life on board the Ship as good as we possibly can for everyone—Crew and civilians alike. Unfortunately, we're always faced with the challenge of balancing those desires against our precious and limited resources. Every gram of consumable mass we spend making the equipment here safer means one less gram which can be used for the fighters and ammo which protect the Ship. Every moment we spend improving this facility is one less moment we can spend caring for others which are more critical and often in even more dire need of maintenance."

"I understand, sir, but it sure seems like the balance of those resources is tipped mightily towards the needs of the Crew. You should have seen the look on your face when the Marine suggested you eat a nutripellet. To you that is a disgusting fate not worth contemplating, while for Nolly and me it is a rare treat beyond measure. The boy would probably have been even more ecstatic about them if he didn't already have an apple in his belly given to him by Cadet Zax earlier today. The cadet thought nothing about gifting a piece of fruit and was genuinely shocked to hear it was the first the child had ever seen in his entire life."

Kalare gasped at that last line, and it also managed to catch the full attention of Aleron, Westerick, and Salmea. Apparently Zax wasn't the only member of the Crew surprised to learn the civilians' food situation was so different than their own. The Boss smiled, and Zax once again saw the full threat of the man behind the expression.

"Would you have us treat everyone on board equally? Who is more important to the Ship and its Mission—the lowliest cadet who is still wet behind the ears, or the most senior civilian in Waste Systems? The cadet, and it's not even close. What good would be served if the Omegas degraded the effectiveness of the Crew one bit in an effort to make life more comfortable for you civilians? The next alien threat we encounter might finally be the one which overwhelms our ability to defend ourselves, and then we're all dead. Or worse.

"The Crew is the Crew because *we* are the people who are best suited to command this Ship and fulfill its mission. We cannot let *anything* get in the way of that. Would things be better for civilians if we decided it was more effective to develop automation for all of the work you do and put the whole lot of you into cryosleep? Do you know how much time and energy is spent on the care and feeding of ten million civilians? An awful lot. And in return we're thanked with behavior like what we're dealing with today. Like what we've been dealing with for the past year. And countless years past when other civilian agitators stood up and tried to question the way things are done. The best and brightest minds on this Ship, descended from the best and brightest of Earth, have been running things just fine for five thousand years. That civilian who keeps getting on the vidscreen to blather at us—what gives him the nerve to think somehow he knows better? Why would any civilian in his right mind have the temerity to think anything like that?"

Imair was unfazed by either the man's words or his tone and pushed ahead.

"You say things are running fine, sir? Look around us. Does this place look like it's fine? Everywhere I go around the Ship it seems critical systems are nearing the end of their useful lifespan. You want to consider automating all of the work civilians do? We could pull *another* ten million people out of cryosleep, put them to work tomorrow, and the maintenance teams would still not be able to fix everything already broken—much less stay on top of the new breakdowns which happen every day. And you think you can somehow automate all of that away with the resources and technology we have available? The best and brightest of Earth may have designed this Ship, sir, but they weren't smart enough to foresee its Mission would be measured in thousands of years rather than hundreds."

Imair had crossed the line. The Boss tolerated her initial barbs, but his expression revealed she had finally pushed him past the breaking point. Having once experienced the officer's full wrath, Zax feared for the civilian. Especially given the current circumstances where nearly any reaction by the Boss, up to and including ordering Bailee to just shoot her, could be easily rationalized. Before the Omega could speak, the image on the vidscreens around the cavern was replaced by a picture of Earth and a civilian's voice emanated from them once more.

"Greetings to the Crew and my fellow civilians. I've come back to you with promising news."

CHAPTER TWENTY-FIVE

Peace is at hand.

"Since we last spoke, I've connected with the Captain to work on an agreement that would allow us to move foward in peace. Although our discussions are not yet finalized, I'm confident they will soon be complete."

Although the voice coming across the vidscreen was disguised to match the earlier one and the person was speaking as if he or she was indeed the same person, Zax was convinced it was someone different. Something about the vocal patterns was unfamiliar and didn't match the earlier announcements. In the end, it didn't matter who was talking on behalf of the civilians as long as *someone* was trying to put an end to the conflict.

"The Captain has requested access to the communication systems so her Crew can hear from her firsthand. Although we've blocked her ability to broadcast up until now, as a sign of good faith I'm going to open up a channel for the Captain now. But I will take a moment to remind her that if the statement strays from the parameters we've discussed, I'll be forced to shut her down. Of course, such action on her part would also represent a serious setback to the negotiations we've all worked so hard to move forwards."

The picture of Earth on the vidscreens faded away and was replaced with the Captain. Zax thought she looked as unflappable as always, though the scar on her throat seemed to be a little more vivid today than he generally remembered.

"I would like to offer my heartfelt thanks to the civilians who my team and I have been speaking with in an effort to come to an agreement which will end this conflict.

"I'm pleased to announce that peace is at hand. Our negotiations are at least halfway complete, and I fully expect they'll be completely wrapped up within the next 240 mins. During this time, I implore the Crew to avoid any conflict with the civilians. Get to a safe place and stay there.

"Though I'll be very frank and say I disagree with their methods, after a great deal of discussion with their leader I have a far greater appreciation for the position the civilians have adopted. This does

not excuse the violence which has occurred, but it sufficiently explains it.

"Where do we stand? The good news is that although there was significant destruction and loss of life in the period which immediately followed the FTL jump, there has been very little since. This has been a painful detour on the long path of the Ship's Mission, but I believe we'll come out the other end stronger for having experienced it.

"In closing, I would like to reiterate one more time. Peace is at hand."

The Captain faded out and her image was once again replaced with that of the human spacecraft. Zax looked around and almost everyone seemed quite pleased at the news their ordeal would soon be over. The notable exception was the Boss who appeared troubled as he stood to speak.

"I need to speak with Sergeant Bailee, Zax, and Kalare, in private. The rest of you, please move over near the workstations."

Aleron and the Waste Systems officers stood and walked away without question. Imair looked confused, but she gathered up Nolly and his box of nutripellets and followed the Omega's instruction. Once she was well out of hearing range, the Boss spoke.

"The Captain just announced she will vent the Ship to clear out all of the civilians and end this uprising. We have 120 mins to reach a compartment near Primary Grav Control. The Omega safe room hidden there is the closest location we should be able to reach which will be among those spared from the venting."

There was stunned silence after the Flight Boss stopped speaking. Zax worried about the officer's mental state after his injury and the anesthesia, but there was zero chance of him questioning the man. Kalare eventually worked up the courage to speak up.

"I'm sorry, sir, but is there any chance you're still feeling side effects from the sedatives? That's the opposite of what the Captain just said."

The Boss smiled. "I understand your hesitancy, Kalare. Yes, the Captain's words were very different from what I just described, but I have accurately conveyed their true meaning. Civilians have mutinied in the Ship's past, so the Omegas have long established contingencies for handling a situation like this. A key component of those plans is to warn the Omegas to move the Crew to safety if at all possible, and the civilian leader was kind enough to provide the Captain with that opportunity. She twice stated her clear intention to forcibly halt the revolt.

"In 119 mins the Bridge will utilize their emergency overrides to disable primary and secondary life support throughout the Ship. They will disable the emergency bulkhead system, override the local controls to force open all of the interior hatches, and then bypass the safeties to prop open every exterior airlock. Everyone and everything which is not secured will get sucked through the massive vacuum that is created and expelled into space. Once that is done, the Marines will fan out across the Ship to dispose of anyone who survived all of that."

Zax was amazed such a plan was even possible and could be put into motion by a handful of Crew working from the Bridge. Then he remembered the stack of cases carefully arranged around the Engineering compartment.

"Sir, what about all of the civilians' bombs?"

"You're right, Zax, the bombs will cause some problems—particularly since they've been coupled to dead man switches. Maybe we'll be lucky enough that a lot of the explosives will get expelled from the Ship along with the civilians they're rigged to before they go off. Even in the best outcome, there will be a lot of Crew casualties as a result of this plan. With all of the bombs in the mix, we'll likely face a lot of catastrophic damage as well. Regardless, the Captain has determined this is our only chance to end this uprising, and I know she would never make that decision lightly. We now have 118 mins to get to the safe room. The rest of the group can join us as well, but I wanted to keep the reason we're leaving secret. Bailee—gather the officers and cadet and make up some story about why we are moving out. Zax—you do the same with the civilians. As much as I would prefer to leave them here, I have no choice but to bring them in order to prevent anyone from learning I'm still around."

Zax stood and watched as Sergeant Bailee approached and said something quietly to the Boss. The Omega nodded in reply, and the Marine turned and walked away while mumbling. Talking to himself was extremely uncharacteristic of the Marine, but perhaps it was a sign that he was human after all and finally exhibiting the effects of fatigue and injury.

Zax called out for Imair and Nolly and gestured for the two to rush back. Imair apparently made a game out of it as they both came running up to Zax giggling like it had been a race. Imair leaned in to talk to Zax quietly.

"Sir—where's everyone going? Shouldn't we wait here based on what the Captain just announced? Especially since the Flight Boss shouldn't even be up and moving yet?"

"That's what I thought too, Imair, but the Boss has a different idea." Zax sighed exaggeratedly to help sell the story he was spinning. "He thinks we'll be safer in a different compartment. I think he's just sick of smelling and looking at all of the crap. Doesn't matter. I gave up trying to understand officers years ago."

Imair smiled and bent down to explain to the boy how they would be heading elsewhere. Zax turned and saw the Boss was watching him. The officer caught his eye and motioned for Zax to come over.

"What did you tell her?"

"I gave her a line about how crazy officers can be, sir."

The Boss genuinely smiled at Zax. "That's good, Zax. Really good. I'm guessing it isn't actually too far from what you see as the truth."

"No comment, sir."

The officer laughed, but then became serious. "Our destination is one level above Primary Grav Control. Can you describe for me the route you're going to take to get us there."

Zax closed his eyes as he visualized the journey and described it to the Omega.

"The first part will be similar to when we made our way up to Waste Systems Control, sir. When we get into the level where we found Nolly, we'll have to leave the maintenance network for a short period so we can get into another network of tunnels. We can stay in that second network to reach the destination."

When Zax opened his eyes, he saw the Boss was looking thoughtful. "Will we go by that ladder where the boy got upset?"

"Yes, sir, but we won't have to go anywhere near that group of civilians he was worried about. Assuming they really existed and were actually in the place he thought they were."

The Omega was quiet for a moment. "Thank you, Zax. That sounds like a good plan. I need you to stay focused on the end game here. Remember—keep doing what you're doing to protect me, and I'm going to make sure you get taken care of when it's all over. OK?"

After all of the time he had spent choking back vomit in the treatment cavern, Zax had warmed up tremendously to the notion of saving the Boss and getting his career back on track. He nodded and said, "Yes, sir."

The Boss raised his voice. "Same formation as earlier, people. Move out."

CHAPTER TWENTY-SIX

I know exactly what I'm doing.

The group left the cavern and their trip upwards was similar to the first time they had made the journey. The biggest difference was having two injured members in their party rather than one. The Boss's wound began bleeding again fairly quickly due to all of the exertion.

Eventually, they reached the portal where they needed to exit the first group of maintenance tunnels and make their way to a different network. The main passageways remained empty. Zax was about to lead them past the ladder where Nolly had earlier warned them about the group of civilians when the Boss called a halt.

"I've decided on a change of plans. Moving around with this many people is too unwieldy, so I want to split up into two groups. Group one is going to be Westerick and Salmea plus the Engineering cadet. I want you three to take this ladder and make your way to Waste Systems Control via the main passageways. Wait there until you receive further orders. The rest of us will carry on to our original destination."

Zax was confused. "But, sir…"

"Leave this to me, cadet. I know exactly what I'm doing."

The Boss's tone made it abundantly clear he did not want any discussion of the matter, but Zax was left dumbfounded as he tried to make sense of the man's order. The officer was sending three members of the Crew to a certain death. Either they would get killed by the group of civilians which Nolly had earlier warned were waiting between the top of the ladder and Waste Systems Control, or they would perish along with so many others when the Captain vented the Ship.

Zax was conflicted. If he had been presented with any reason to push back against the Boss earlier in the day, he would have done so without thinking twice out of general principle. Now, with the opportunity to get his career on the proper trajectory again, his calculus was different. It wasn't as if the man was trying to shed Kalare or Sergeant Bailee.

Zax looked over at Westerick and Salmea. The major appeared nervous at the idea of leaving the relative safety of the larger group, but there was no way the man was going to question the Boss about the matter. Salmea, as always, seemed indifferent. Zax tried to dredge up compassion for the officers and the fate he expected for them if they left the main group. After working with them for a year, however, he had a hard time putting himself at any risk only to help them continue their incompetent service. Zax was still debating whether or not to further question the Boss's change in plans when Kalare spoke up.

"Respectfully, sir, I suggest the cadet stay with us rather than go with the officers. I understand your intentions, sir, but I believe keeping him close will prove useful later on today. Once all of this is over, we will need to get Engineering cleaned up and back to normal as fast as possible."

Zax had been conflicted about Westerick and Salmea but hadn't given a second thought to Aleron walking off to his doom. He was dismayed to hear Kalare jump to the bully's defense. What could she be thinking? She was well aware the boy had tormented Zax his entire life. In fact, she had been attacked or threatened by the idiot herself on multiple occasions. What would possess Kalare to want to keep Aleron around? Then Zax thought back to some of the interactions he had witnessed between the two of them over the past few hours. If Aleron was getting chummy with Kalare, it must surely be yet another in the long list of ways the boy schemed to hurt Zax. He clearly deserved whatever fate awaited at the other end of that ladder.

A final glance at Aleron triggered different feelings. Zax took a moment to really look at his classmate, and even though it was nearly impossible to see past a lifetime's worth of bullying, the boy was just that—a boy. An idiot boy, but still someone who was trying to figure out his place in life and the Crew just like Zax was. He didn't deserve to get tossed aside and left for dead. Zax knew he would probably regret the choice some day, but decided he couldn't watch the cadet get sent off to his demise.

"I wholeheartedly agree with Kalare, sir."

The Boss's eyes flared with anger at Kalare's suggestion and Zax's agreement, but the man's expression softened once he took a long look at Zax and Kalare. He finally nodded his approval before addressing the Waste Systems officers.

"Major—you appear apprehensive about walking off on your own. I understand I'm asking a lot by splitting you from the rest of our group. Sergeant Bailee—hand the major your blaster."

The Marine looked unfazed about giving away their only weapon and handed it to Westerick without hesitation. The major's demeanor changed instantly once the blaster was in his hand. He stood up straighter and there was a glint in his eye. Zax could not understand why the Boss would put himself and everyone else in the main travel party at risk only to provide the major a little comfort. The Boss continued.

"We never saw any civilians in this part of Waste Systems, so I have to imagine things will be empty where you're going, but I want you to feel safe. If you run into any civilians, though, your orders are to fire immediately. Is that clear?"

"Sir, yes, sir," the major responded as his chest puffed out with bravado.

The last order made the Boss's rationale in giving away the blaster clear to Zax. The Omega wanted to be certain that if Westerick and Salmea ran into civilians, they wouldn't be tempted to take their chances and surrender. Once the major was armed, the Boss knew he would fight. The most likely outcome given the major's incompetence would be the death of the two officers at the hands of the civilians with no risk of them being questioned and giving up the Omega's presence in the area. Zax rationalized away his apprehension about the officers' fate as this outcome was probably a more humane way for them to die versus being vented into space along with everyone else.

"Now I'm stuck getting dragged around on the Boss's little adventure instead of waiting this thing out in safety with those two. Thanks for nothing, you useless oxygen thief."

Aleron had approached and whispered in Zax's ear while the Waste Systems officers received their final orders from the Boss. The bully then brushed past roughly, jamming an elbow into Zax's belly and stomping a boot on his foot in the process. Zax found it amazing how he regretted the decision to save the boy's life even faster than he could have imagined, but the choice was made and there was no going back. They all watched the officers disappear up the ladder and then the Boss spoke.

"Let's move."

Zax led the group through a series of turns until they reached the access port for the next set of maintenance tunnels. He was about to seal the hatch behind them when he heard a series of blaster shots off in the distance back from where they had come. Zax strained to hear if the noise repeated, but there was only silence. He shut the hatch.

CHAPTER TWENTY-SEVEN

I'll carry the boy.

The smaller group moved through the next set of tunnels faster than they had been able to previously. As they went upwards towards Primary Grav Control, the air became tinged with the smell of something burning. The odor became more intense as they ascended and Zax eventually halted the group once its source became clear.

They had turned a corner and stared into the gaping maw of a blast hole. It appeared to have swallowed not only the control room but also the passageways and maintenance tunnels which surrounded it. The explosion had been so strong there weren't any recognizable human remains in sight, but the fact many people had died here was abundantly clear from the overwhelming smell of cooked flesh.

The heat of the blast had been so intense that some of the surfaces closest to the center of the detonation still glowed red. The tunnel was sheared so it now opened up into a main passageway, but the path forward was on the other side of a five-meter wide fissure which was at least thirty meters deep. The Boss looked at Zax after surveying the situation.

"Cadet—what are our options?"

Zax visualized the layout of the nearby passageways and tunnels. "There aren't any great ones, sir. There's an access port a few hundred meters back which can put us into the main passageways, but looking at all of this damage, it appears we'll just get blocked again when we try to reach our target. The only clear path I see requires going down a dozen levels and will add 23 mins to the journey."

The Omega pondered Zax's words for a few moments as he looked around. Eventually, he shook his head. "No—we can't risk backtracking when we're so close. Who knows what we might encounter along the way. We need to figure out something e6lse. I need ideas, people."

There was silence as everyone looked around and considered what appeared to be an insurmountable obstacle. Finally, Aleron spoke.

"I got it, sir! Look at all of the fiber optic cable that got exposed by the blast. There's some right over there, and another huge tangle of it above us. If we can figure out something to use as a hook, we can pull down the cable above us and if it's still solidly anchored, we can use it to swing across this gap!"

Zax looked up and saw how the plan might work. Someone once told Zax there was enough fiber optic cable strung throughout the Ship to span the distance between Earth and its moon a dozen times. Its ubiquity in the wreckage had initially made the many tangles of cable fade into the background.

The Boss smiled at Aleron. "That may be the craziest idea I've ever heard, cadet, but it just might work. Keeping you around is already paying off. Grab that cable from over there—I see some metal over here which might work as a hook."

The Boss walked over to what appeared to be the remnants of a workstation blown out of the control room. One of the drawers had been blasted into a hunk of twisted metal but was shaped such that Zax could immediately recognize how the Omega wanted to use it. A few minutes later the metal had been bent into a rough hook and attached to a piece of cable. Aleron swung it in an arc next to his body and after three attempts he snagged some of the cable from the tangled mass above their heads. He gave a few tugs and eventually worked loose a long loop that he pulled down within reach. He gave a few hard tugs and then looked around.

"Someone needs to go first. Since it was my idea, it might as well be me."

Without pausing, he walked back a couple of paces and then bolted towards the chasm. Zax held his breath as Aleron swung across the gap and then dropped to a perfect landing on the opposite side. The cable swung back and Sergeant Bailee grabbed hold and then looked at the group.

"Kalare's going next, then I will go, then the civilians, and then the Boss and Zax."

Kalare gulped as she approached the Marine and grabbed the cable. She backed up as far as the cable would allow and then took off at full speed. Her hands visibly slipped as she crossed the midpoint of the arc, but she held on long enough to fall into Aleron's waiting arms on the other side. She smiled up at him and remained in his embrace a few beats too long for Zax's comfort.

Bailee made it look easy as he used his sole good arm to hang on. Zax had taken his place at the edge and caught the cable as it swung back. He handed it off to Imair and she made it look even easier than the Marine had. Zax caught the cable once again on its return and motioned for Nolly to approach the edge.

"OK, Nolly, you saw how everyone else did this. Looks like a lot of fun, right?"

The young civilian trembled like a trip across the fissure was his worst nightmare. He stood at the edge and his eyes went wide and brimmed with tears as he stared into the wreckage below. Imair called out from the other side.

"You can do it, Nolly. I'll be right here to catch you, OK? I know how strong you are. This will be super easy for you."

The boy shook his head. Just once at first, but then repeatedly as he backed away from the edge. He kept backing up without looking until he crashed against the Boss's legs. Zax had been focused on Nolly the entire time, and he looked up at the Boss expecting the man to be livid. Instead, the Omega had a warm smile on his face. He dropped to a knee and spoke softly to the boy.

"You know, I'm terrified of heights so I've been getting super nervous watching everyone else swinging across that big hole. It looks pretty scary to me. I think I would feel a lot better if I could have someone ride with me. Do you think you could climb on my back and hold on tight to keep me company and help me not be afraid?"

Zax stared with his jaw slack. It was one of the most sweet and tender displays he had ever seen from anyone in the Crew, and it was coming from the Boss. Nolly's terror had rendered him mute, but he managed to nod his agreement. The Boss looked up at Zax.

"I'll carry the boy. You go next."

"Yes, sir."

Zax backed up and ran as fast as he could. He was two-thirds of the way to the point where he intended to let go of the cable when it came slightly loose from whatever anchored it above and slipped a half a meter. Zax had been on track to stick a perfect landing, but the cable slippage threw him off balance. He landed instead in a twisted heap at Kalare's feet and let loose a stream of curses. She laughed so riotously that even Sergeant Bailee couldn't avoid a smile.

Zax stood up and saw the Boss had caught the cable on its return and held it firmly in both hands. Nolly was perched on the officer's back with his arms locked so firmly around the man's throat they threatened to squeeze the life out of him. The Omega backed up and then sprinted towards the edge where he leapt for the far side.

The full combined mass of the Boss and Nolly on the cable forced something to finally give way up in the bundle of tangles it emanated from. The Boss had already established enough angular momentum that he didn't instantly plummet downwards, but rather than arcing over the edge of the chasm to land with everyone else, he crashed into the wreckage just inside the fissure.

In a flash, everyone peered over the edge and saw the Boss's predicament. He clung to the side with the barest of handholds as the cable unspooled uselessly into the crater below. The group looked at each other as they each thought about out how to save the officer and child without access to all of the additional cable on the other side of the divide. Imair rushed forward and pointed at Zax and Kalare.

"You two—grab my legs and lower me down. We can pull them up!"

The two cadets held tight as Imair dangled into the chasm. A moment later she yelled for them to lift and she emerged with Nolly in tow. Once the boy was safely on the deck, she went over again for the Boss. Zax held with all his might but felt the civilian's leg slipping from his grasp once she was also supporting the officer's mass. Sergeant Bailee saw the impending disaster and reached down with his one functional arm to grab a handful of waist from the back of Imair's pants. Aleron jumped in as well and all four of them hauled the civilian and Omega back up over the edge of the wreckage.

The Boss stood and smiled at the civilian woman as he brushed himself off. "Thank you, Imair."

The civilian grinned at the Boss addressing her by name for the first time during their hours together. "My pleasure, sir. I understand how important it is we keep you alive."

CHAPTER TWENTY-EIGHT

Everyone take a deep breath.

"OK, Zax, how much further?" The Boss still had a flush in his cheeks from his misadventure as he looked at Zax expectantly. With the bomb wreckage behind them, there appeared to be a clear path to the destination. Only a few hundred meters of passageway stood between them and the target compartment, and Zax relayed this information. The officer smiled in response. "We just might make it after all. Everyone—let's move."

The dissipating adrenalin from rescuing the Boss and Nolly combined with the relief of being so close to their final destination resulted in the group moving in more of ragtag fashion than the tight formation they had maintained previously. The three cadets led the way, followed by Nolly and then Imair, with Bailee and finally the Boss bringing up the rear.

They reached a Tube junction which Zax recognized as the last milestone before they would get to the compartment with the safe room. He walked past the useless Tube and a few secs later heard a commotion behind him. He turned and saw Imair had tripped on something and crashed to the deck.

The civilian was not hurt, but she seemed embarrassed and paused for a few secs as she appeared to gather her wits. Sergeant Bailee, uncharacteristically, offered her a hand up once he was close enough, but she brushed it away. The Marine shrugged and walked past her, and Zax turned to move on as well. He had only taken a half dozen steps when he heard the Marine bellow behind him.

"Drop it or I kill the boy!"

Zax spun around and was startled by the tableau before him. Imair had backed herself against the Tube entrance and held the Boss in front of her as a shield with one hand clutched against his wound. She had a mini blaster in the other hand which was pointed at the Omega's temple as he grimaced in pain. Sergeant Bailee knelt a few meters away with his back to Zax. The Marine was crouched behind Nolly to shield himself from Imair and held an identical mini blaster pointed at the boy's head.

The Boss remained perfectly still as he spoke calmly and deliberately.

"Everyone take a deep breath. No one has to get hurt here—especially the boy. Imair—let me go and drop the weapon. You've got nowhere to go. Trust me, you're not getting away from here and killing me won't get you anything. Let me go, drop the weapon, and everything will be OK."

Time seemed to slow down for Zax as he watched what happened next as if in slow motion.

Imair's resolve appeared to waver as she listened to the Boss's words, and she lowered the blaster away from the officer's head. As she did so, the Tube entrance opened behind her. She pointed the weapon at Nolly and pulled the trigger. The blast still echoed in the passage as she yanked the Boss into the Tube, the door shut, and they were gone.

Sergeant Bailee bolted for the Tube and pounded on the entrance to no effect. Nolly remained standing for a moment and looked down at his chest. Then, he crumpled silently, face down, onto the deck. Zax dashed for the boy and got there at the same time as Kalare and Aleron. They rolled the boy onto his back and revealed the massive damage the blaster had done to his small body. He opened his eyes and looked at Zax.

"It hurts so bad, sir."

The boy coughed twice and then his slight frame spasmed for a few secs before going still. Zax checked for a pulse and found none. Nolly was dead.

CHAPTER TWENTY-NINE

You need to look at the big picture.

Zax couldn't comprehend what had just happened in the blink of an eye. He stared quietly for a few secs until it truly sank in. Then he pounded on Nolly's chest in a poor imitation of a medic trying to revive someone's heart.

"No, no, no, NO!"

A strong hand gripped Zax's shoulder and he whirled around. Sergeant Bailee looked down at him with compassion. Zax slapped the Marine's arm aside.

"Don't touch me! This is all your fault! How could you use that boy as a bargaining chip, as a shield? He's eight! What kind of monster tries to save himself at the expense of an eight-year-old? Where the hell did the blasters come from, anyways?"

The Marine remained stoic in the face of Zax's attack.

"The Boss retrieved the blasters from a hidden weapons cache which Omegas can access. He visited it earlier when the two of you were traveling alone. He and I thought it was better to keep their existence a secret in case we needed the element of surprise at some point. She must have discovered the Boss's somehow and took it when she grabbed him.

"As for the boy's death—the woman had absolutely no reason to do so and she killed him anyways. Doesn't it seem like that might have been part of her plan all along? It was probably a distraction to prevent me from taking a shot. Or maybe the boy has some information she wanted to guarantee we didn't get. Or maybe she was just sick and tired of him clinging to her all day long. I have no idea, but it doesn't matter. She killed the boy. More importantly, she has the Boss."

Kalare had sidled over and placed a calming hand on Zax's shoulder. He allowed it to stay but maintained his outrage. "I couldn't care less about him right now! Nolly's dead."

The sergeant sighed loudly. "You want to be a pilot, cadet? You're doing that because you want to be an officer someday and lead, right? Maybe even be an Omega? Well, today's your lucky day. You get the lesson early in your career that so many Flight officers don't get until much later—people die. As part of the Ship's Mission, people die. Some will be people you detest, but some will be people you appreciate. Some will die for good reasons, some for bad. Regardless, your job is to learn from each death and move on as fast as possible.

"I know you're upset because the boy was your friend and he was young. I get all of that. But you have to put that aside and think about the big picture. If she was able to get that Tube to function, it means the woman has been working with the civilian insurgents all along. That means they have the Boss and that's a massive problem which is entirely on me for not killing him before that door shut."

Zax wanted to argue about the importance of Nolly's death but was shocked by the sergeant's words. "Wait—you would have killed the Boss? What is it with you and officers today? First you take out the Chief Engineer and now you turn around and say you were ready to kill the Boss too."

"Big picture, cadet. You need to look at the big picture. What's about to happen here? The Captain is going to shut down the life support system and vent the Ship. Why is she willing to kill ten million civilians and some large portion of our Crew? To prevent the worst possible thing from happening—civilian takeover. This group of civilians is well-prepared compared to those of past attempted revolutions, but like all of the others they don't have a truly effective bargaining chip. The Captain needs to guarantee they don't get one."

Aleron's eyes had gone wide at the mention of the Ship being vented. He opened his mouth to say something, but quickly closed it rather than interrupt the sergeant as the man continued.

"In the big picture no one cares if they bomb a bunch of compartments and kill hundreds or even thousands of Crew. We can replace everyone on this Ship and *almost* everything. What is the only thing on this Ship that is truly irreplaceable?"

The Marine looked at each of the cadets and waited. Kalare removed her hand from Zax's shoulder and broke the silence.

"The FTL."

The Marine smiled. "If I gave a damn about credits, you'd have just earned a bunch. The FTL engine is the only thing on this Ship which we can neither repair nor replace. That's why it's isolated and protected the way it is. The civilians managed to pierce the first layers of security and got into Engineering. But they're still blocked by the impenetrable armor which surrounds the FTL compartment.

"Only four Omegas have the security permissions necessary to access that compartment. The Captain, the Boss, the Chief Engineer, and a fourth who is known to Alpha and only identified if the other three are incapacitated in an emergency. Each of those officers has been trained to withstand nearly inhuman levels of pain, but every person has a breaking point. Who knows what kind of crazy torture is possible with these collars patched into our Plugs. Killing the Chief Engineer was the only way to guarantee she never gave the civilians access to the FTL. She knew we would try to do it and almost certainly welcomed the reprieve from the torture she faced."

Aleron finally got up the nerve to jump in. "I don't get it, Sergeant. What benefit would the civilians have from getting access to the FTL? They would be just as screwed as the Crew if they destroyed it. We'd all be stuck on this stupid rock in the middle of nowhere, unable to reach anywhere else before running out of fuel."

"Good point, cadet, but in the big picture they have nothing to lose. If you already believe you've hit absolute bottom, then even something as insane as marooning the Ship for all eternity is a rational strategy. The Captain is no doubt well aware of this dynamic which is why she's willing to take the drastic action of venting the Ship.

"The game theory changes once they have the Boss, though. That's one crazy tough man, but eventually he'll crack. Everyone cracks—it's just a question of how long it takes. Once he does, the civilians will access the FTL compartment and load it up with explosives. A legitimate threat of FTL destruction will guarantee them the upper hand, and the Captain will have no choice but to surrender and give the civilians whatever they want."

The cadets were quiet for a few secs as they processed the Marine's words. The pause allowed Zax to recognize why he had reacted so viscerally to Bailee's statement about killing the Boss. It was not driven by any concern for the officer's well-being, but instead by what Zax feared it would mean for the nascent recovery of his career. The harsh reality of Nolly's death combined with the sergeant's revelations about the high stakes involved in their situation finally made everything click into place. Any worries about his career were absurd in the middle of this revolution. If the civilians managed to wrest control of the Ship, the whole idea of credits and the Leaderboard would be moot. Yes—the person who spoke on their behalf said the civilians wouldn't change things once they were in control, but Zax had to believe that was a lie. Why else would the Omegas be so afraid of civilian control that the Captain would be willing to vent the Ship and kill almost everyone rather than let them have it?

One thing nagged at Zax about the Marine's explanation. "Excuse me, Sergeant, but if the Captain is about to vent the Ship, why does this matter at all? Surely the Boss can manage to hold out against even the worst torture knowing it will all be over soon enough."

"You would be right, cadet, except for one important thing. When they vent the Ship, there are certain critical compartments which will be excluded. The Bridge, Engineering, safe rooms like the one we were trying to reach, Marine garrisons, and a few others. Even after the Ship has been mostly purged, the civilians will remain in control of Engineering and continue to work on the Boss. If they are smart, and all indications suggest they are, they will throw everything they can at keeping us out of that compartment until the Boss cracks and they access the FTL."

The Marine waited for his last revelation to sink in. Eventually, Kalare spoke up.

"So how are we going to kill the Boss before that happens?"

Sergeant Bailee smiled. "I thought you'd never ask. Corporal—lift your visor."

CHAPTER THIRTY

I need you out of that suit, Corporal.

Aleron and Kalare gaped as a disembodied face appeared and floated next to Sergeant Bailee. Zax, already familiar with the capabilities of ChamWare after his previous adventure with the Marines, smiled in recognition. The presence of this Marine who had been invisible thanks to his chameleon suit finally explained some of the odd behaviors by the Boss and the sergeant which Zax had noticed earlier. The corporal addressed Bailee.

"Sergeant—the Boss was in my way so I couldn't shoot at first. I had almost moved into position for a clean headshot on the woman when the Tube opened. They were gone before I could react."

"Understood, Corporal, that took me by surprise too. Beyond the fact it's been shut down through all of this, who would've ever imagined civilians gaining access to the Tube. Fully disengage your camouflage." The corporal closed his eyes for a moment to interface with his Plug and then his entire body materialized next to Bailee. The Marine was carrying a standard blaster and also had a mini blaster in a holster on his hip. He appeared to be almost the same height and weight as the sergeant. Bailee looked the man up and down and smiled.

"I was hoping we'd be about the same size. The fact you're carrying a mini blaster is a huge bonus. I need you out of that suit, Corporal."

The Marine hesitated. "Begging the Sergeant's pardon, but your arm—"

"I need you out of that suit, now, Corporal." Bailee's tone made it clear there would be no further discussion, so the younger Marine started to remove the ChamWare. The first step in this process was removing his holster which he handed over to the sergeant. Bailee accepted the weapon and turned to present it to Zax.

"I thought I'd be forced to give you the blaster rifle, but thankfully we managed to connect with a Marine who breaks regulations and carries an unauthorized sidearm. It's a pretty stupid regulation, so I'm glad he's smart enough to disregard it. This mini blaster can be disengaged from the ChamWare and remain invisible for a few hours, but doing so limits it to firing only two shots because the rest of the energy charge is needed to maintain the camouflage.

"I'm going to get into this Marine's suit and then you and I are going to doubletime it to Engineering. I'm certain that's where the Boss is headed, so you need to get us back in there again. There's no way they'll be stupid enough to let us take a shot at him the way we took out the Chief Engineer earlier, but hopefully the suit will let me take them by surprise. Worst case, you'll have the mini blaster. You need to be sure you don't let them find it, even when they frisk you, so you can take the shot if they manage to incapacitate me. Understood, cadet?"

Zax was at a loss for words. If someone had handed him a blaster and ordered him to kill the Boss earlier that day, he would have done so with a smile. But having seen the gruesome aftermath of blaster shots up close with the Chief Engineer and Nolly, Zax's stomach dropped at the thought of pulling a trigger and being responsible for that outcome.

He had also become entirely conflicted about the Boss, and this wasn't solely due to self-interest. Zax still felt the man was likely responsible for Mikedo's death, but Kalare's exhortations over the past year combined with the Omega's behavior during their time together had created sufficient doubt that Zax no longer took this as a certainty. But if the sergeant was telling him that killing the Boss was necessary to save the Ship, then Zax had to believe him. He took a deep breath and finally nodded in response to the Marine's question.

"Wait," whined Aleron, "what about us? Are we supposed to just sit here and wait for the Captain to vent us out into space?"

The sergeant looked like he desperately wanted to punch Aleron again. It was amazing how the cadet brought out that reaction in so many people. "I can't bring the three of you with us because I bet they would never let all of you get near the Boss—especially a Marine. I'm betting that if Zax shows up and appears to be by himself, there's a chance they let him get near the man. Corporal—can you take my blaster and escort these two cadets to a Marine garrison?"

"Yes, Sergeant. I'll get them there."

"OK, it's settled then. Once I'm suited up Zax and I will head to Engineering, and you three will head to a garrison. Hopefully, you can get there before the Captain vents the Ship, but if we don't manage to kill the Boss, you might actually be better off if you don't."

CHAPTER THIRTY-ONE

The fate of the Ship is in your hands right now.

The three cadets watched as the corporal helped with the final steps required to get Bailee into the ChamWare. Trying to suit up with a nearly useless arm proved challenging for the older Marine, but he accepted the assistance only begrudgingly. Aleron reached for the kit bag at one point in an effort to be useful, but a withering look from the sergeant made the boy retreat a few paces down the passageway to observe from a safer distance. Kalare pulled Zax aside and leaned in close for a quiet chat.

"How do you feel about all of this, Zax?"

"Sick. Just sick."

"Do you think you can really pull the trigger and kill the Boss?"

Zax closed his eyes and sucked in a couple of calming breaths. His comment about feeling sick was not entirely figurative, but the emptiness of his stomach thankfully kept Puke Boy from visiting. Zax opened his eyes, but he looked down at the deck rather than make eye contact with Kalare. "Hopefully it never comes to that. I think the plan is that I'm a decoy and just need to get the sergeant into position. He'll be the one that takes the shot."

"I know that's the plan, but you have to be sure you're prepared to do it too. Killing someone is not easy. I was lucky earlier. I had no time to think about what I was doing with that civilian who was guarding us. It was an obvious choice between watching you die or stabbing him, and thankfully my training took over in the moment and made it easy."

Kalare paused for a moment and took a deep breath before continuing. "But I've been reliving it ever since, and I'm completely nauseous about it. That makes me even more worried about you. I know how you obsess over things, and I'm sure you're already looking at this from ten different angles. If you let too many doubts creep in, your subconscious is going to get in the way when it comes time to shoot and either make you hesitate or make you miss. You can't let that happen. You heard what's at stake. The fate of the Ship is in your hands right now. You *must* take that shot. You *must* kill the Boss if you get the chance."

Zax wanted to assure Kalare that he could do what was being asked of him but knew he'd be lying.

He hoped he would pull the trigger if needed, but he had absolutely no idea whether or not he really could. He was trying to figure out the best way to explain how conflicted he felt when suddenly Bailee's face floated next to Kalare's. She was startled and Zax laughed. The Marine cracked the slightest smile and then addressed Zax.

"Cadet—we need to move out. There isn't much time left before the Captain puts her plan into motion. If we get delayed and aren't in Engineering before that happens, the Ship is lost."

The Marine's head bounced away for a few final words with the corporal. Zax looked at Kalare to say goodbye and saw how her brilliant blue eyes shimmered with tears. He wanted to reassure her that everything would be fine, but opening his mouth might unleash his own emotions. He gave her a quick hug instead and immediately turned to walk down the passageway.

As Zax passed Aleron, the bigger boy reached out and put a hand on his shoulder. He spun towards the bully expecting one last torment but instead found that the boy wore a gentle smile.

"I wanted to say thanks, Zax, for what you did earlier. I realize now how you and Kalare saved me from getting vented by convincing the Boss to keep me around. Thank you. Good luck."

Zax was still unable to speak, so he simply nodded in reply and resumed walking. A moment later he saw the Marine's head bobbing along beside him out of the corner of his eye. They turned a corner and Bailee ordered a stop a few meters later.

"Let's discuss the plan, cadet. How are you going to get us back into Engineering?"

"A couple hundred meters ahead is a series of tunnels which will connect with the ones we used earlier and eventually get us there, Sergeant."

"What happens when we arrive? What options do we have for accessing the area around the main Engineering Control compartment?"

"Not many, Sergeant. There are a couple of different hatches that will put us into the various smaller rooms like the ones where we were held earlier. There's also an access port about 50 meters away from the main entrance. Of course there's also the hatch inside the main compartment which we used when you took care of the Chief Engineer earlier."

Zax had intentionally softened his language about the fate of the Chief Engineer having heard the rationale from the Marine, but he feared his tone still likely betrayed his distaste about what had happened to the woman. The sergeant had no reaction other than to stare ahead for a moment as he considered their options.

"I think tackling this head on is probably our best bet. Let's drop straight into the main compartment again unless something happens between now and then to suggest a better plan." The Marine's face disappeared as he lowered the visor of his suit. "I'm going to walk 5 meters ahead and to your right, cadet. Do your best to not shoot me in the back if we encounter any civilians before we reach the tunnels."

Zax started walking and found himself immediately brooding about what would happen once they reached Engineering Control. He needed to mentally prepare for the scenario where he got the Boss in his sights and had to pull the trigger. Every time he envisioned that outcome, however, his mind flashed back to memories of how the Chief looked once Bailee shot her. His memory of that moment played back on a slow-motion loop of blood and gore. Could he do that to anyone, much less someone he knew well like the Boss?

He was so deep into a trance of worry that Zax didn't immediately notice the two civilians who approached from the other end of the passageway as he turned a corner. They were ten meters away and raised their blasters in response to his appearance. Zax still had the mini blaster in his hand and instinctually raised it to point at the civilians. He realized he should shoot immediately given the element of surprise provided by the invisible blaster, but he couldn't bring himself to pull the trigger. His mind spun uselessly and he kept waiting to hear Bailee open fire. The invisible Marine's blaster remained silent for some reason as Zax thought, *"Where the hell did Bailee go?"*

CHAPTER THIRTY-TWO

Don't let her get away!

The male civilian held his blaster ready and appeared apprehensive as they approached Zax, but the female lowered hers and started to laugh.

"Look, how cute. The cadet's going to pretend to shoot us with his make believe blaster. I might *almost* feel bad about killing this one." She raised her free hand and made a blaster shape with her thumb and forefinger which she pointed at Zax as she advanced. "Looks like we have a standoff," she said and then chuckled.

Zax's heart pounded in his throat. He knew he needed to pull the trigger, but his finger seemed a million klicks away and refused to respond to his commands. Nine meters. Eight meters. The civilians marched closer and closer, and the woman's mocking laughter became more and more raucous.

Two blaster shots rang out in quick succession. They came from 5 meters ahead and to Zax's right— exactly where Sergeant Bailee had said he would be. The first blast killed the male civilian instantly and he crumbled to the deck. The second blew the woman's blaster apart and shattered her leg in the process. She screamed in a combination of shock and pain as she spun away and collapsed. She furiously clawed with her arms and kicked with her uninjured leg to scramble down the passage away from them.

"Cadet—shoot her! Don't let her get away!"

The Marine's words bounced around the passageway, but Zax quickly realized the echo effect was being created by his own mind and its distorted perception of time passing. His invisible blaster remained perfectly aimed as his vision tunneled and he focused on the center of the fleeing woman's back. His finger tightened on the trigger, but each gram of pressure required ever increasing willpower. The woman approached the far corner where she would escape out of sight. Zax closed his eyes and pleaded with his body to shoot, but his finger would move no further.

A moment later his eyes popped opened involuntarily at the roar of the Marine's blaster. The woman collapsed face down on the deck—lifeless. Zax was still standing with his unused blaster pointed down the passageway and his mouth agape when he felt an invisible palm strike his face. The force of the slap sent him sprawling to the ground. Zax dropped the weapon and some small part of his mind appreciated how its invisibility function automatically switched off as it hit the deck and bounced away. The majority of his brain focused on the pain that reverberated through his body. His cheek felt like it was on fire, and Zax noticed a coppery taste which signaled his lip had been split by the blow.

"What is your malfunction, boy?" The Marine lifted his visor and the scarlet flush which accompanied the sergeant's rage was even more impressive than usual as his face hovered disembodied only a few inches away. "You let those two practically walk right up and grab you! You couldn't even be bothered to take the shot when I served the woman up to you on a platter! I wouldn't expect anything better out of a typical Flight puke, but you've been through Marine training! Did we not beat it into you strongly enough?"

Zax flashed back to his weeks of training at the hands of the Marines prior to his planetary expedition. They had indeed beaten their ethos and many essential capabilities into him fairly well. Zax excelled at battling other cadets with non-lethal ammunition and performed even better during his live fire exercise against a series of hostile bots. Those weren't nearly the same thing as this, however. He had never been faced with the challenge of killing a living being. Even during Landfall he never had an opportunity to shoot at the hostile aliens. The ability that most separated the Marines from Flight was how they looked at an enemy up close and took direct action to snuff out a life. Yes—Zax may have been trained by the Marines and trained well, but he had never practiced their most crucial skill.

He opened his mouth to explain this to the enraged Marine, but no words came out. Zax was instead overwhelmed by emotion and started to sob. It wasn't the pain from the slap, the shame of failure, or his residual fear, but a toxic stew of all three.

The Marine backed away, though it appeared to be out of disgust more than compassion. It was almost as if the man worried the emotion might be contagious. He allowed Zax to choke out the tears for a min but spoke again before they had a chance to subside.

"I know this is hard, cadet, but I don't have time to nurse you along and help you process all of it. The fate of the Ship will be decided by our actions *right now*. The plan is that I will take the shot and kill the Boss, but you must get your head right and be prepared to do it as well. The civilians in Engineering will be watching for anything out of the ordinary. If you hesitate for a moment once you lift your blaster, you'll be dead and the Ship will be lost. Do you understand me?"

Zax managed to get his weeping under control while the Marine spoke. He knew he was capable of making any shot and nailing any target. In fact, he might even be a better marksman than the sergeant. The only thing that could get in his way would be his mind, and he resolved that he would not allow it to get the better of him again. Zax would do whatever needed to be done. Period.

He looked up at the Marine and nodded agreement. Zax used his fingers to brush the tears off his cheeks and the back of his sleeve to wipe the copious snot from under his nose. He stood and dusted himself off before walking over to where the blaster had come to rest against the bulkhead. It switched back to invisible mode once he firmly gripped it. Zax stared at the Marine with budding determination and declared, "Let's move."

CHAPTER THIRTY-THREE

Will you actually shoot this time?

Sergeant Bailee drove a punishing pace once they entered the maintenance tunnels and no longer had to fear encountering any civilians. The Marine's preferred method of pushing Zax ever faster was jamming the blaster muzzle into his back with a few sharp barks of "Move your ass!" sprinkled in for good measure. Zax was amazed how quickly the man moved up and down ladders with his arm as damaged as it was. He had to imagine the Marine was in excruciating pain, but the man's ChamWare allowed him to keep any outward expressions of it hidden. He drew inspiration from the Marine's fortitude and endeavored to match him stride for invisible stride.

Zax used the time throughout their journey to focus on getting ready for the challenge ahead. One task he knew would be critical was keeping the blaster hidden from the civilians in Engineering Control once he was back in their grasp. It seemed ironic to worry about hiding an invisible weapon, but it wasn't quite as simple as it might sound. Zax would certainly be thoroughly frisked and, invisible or not, the weapon would be easily felt if it was hidden anywhere on his person.

The best approach seemed to be keeping the weapon in his grip at all times. If his hands appeared to be empty, then the civilians would most likely believe they were. Zax had never known the Ship carried such small weapons with the power of invisibility and believed the civilians wouldn't possess that knowledge either. He practiced holding the weapon while keeping his hand in a relaxed, neutral position that would not give away what it was actually doing.

The fidgeting with his blaster also served a completely different purpose. It gave Zax an outlet for the nervous energy which built up as they got closer and closer to their destination. His failure to shoot at the two civilians when he should have done so weighed heavily on him. It was a solid foundation of nerves upon which ever greater levels of fear were being layered.

Zax fully understood now how his earlier worries about career enhancement were ludicrous. He was marching to a certain death. If either he or Bailee somehow managed to get a shot off and kill the Boss, their success would certainly be met with immediate execution at the hands of enraged civilians. If they failed, then they would suffer the same fate for having made the attempt in the first place.

What kept Zax going was the knowledge that if they succeeded it would give Kalare and the rest of the Crew a chance for a fresh start. Once the Captain vented the Ship, it would be easy enough for the Marines to mop up the remaining resistance. They would quickly thaw out some previously Culled Crew and enough civilians to repopulate the vessel, and they could proceed as if the whole nightmare had never happened.

If they failed, Zax was convinced things would end poorly for the Crew under civilian control. Their leader had announced not much would change as a result of their mutiny, but Zax had zero faith in those words. His dealings with civilians during the day's events had shown how ruthless and cruel they were at their core. From the pile of corpses in Engineering Control to the way Imair killed Nolly to cover her escape, it was clear the insurgents would stop at nothing to achieve their goals. Yes, lots of Crew would die when the Ship was vented, but Zax felt they were better off than they would be if the civilians were allowed to take command. Who knew how the rebels might choose to pay back generations of perceived grudges once they had the power to mercilessly do so. At least the Crew who perished as a result of the venting were guaranteed a reasonably quick and relatively painless death.

They approached the Engineering section and Sergeant Bailee called a halt.

"I still believe dropping into the main compartment is our best bet, but I want to take a few mins to scout out the nearby area. Let's make sure the civilians haven't done anything too tricky and are holding the Boss elsewhere."

"Yes, Sergeant."

At the first compartment they encountered they stopped to listen at the access hatch and heard a maelstrom of voices. There must have been a couple dozen civilians yammering away down below. It was impossible to tell If the Boss was in there among them all without giving themselves away by opening the hatch and taking a peek.

They moved to the second compartment and discovered the same. And the third as well. At each successive hatch, they eavesdropped with the final conclusion being that Engineering had been positively overrun with insurgents in the hours since they had been there earlier. Sergeant Bailee had predicted the civilians would do everything they could to maintain their grip on the critical compartment, and it appeared he had been correct. Hundreds if not thousands of civilians were amassed in an attempt to prevent the Crew from regaining control.

Zax's legs wobbled more and more the higher and higher his silent tally of insurgents climbed. He knew it should make no difference given that he and Sergeant Bailee would bypass them all by dropping directly into Engineering Control, but there was still something about discovering all of the hostiles nearby that made him woozy. An armed, angry mob of civilians was prepared to wreak havoc on the Ship. Thank goodness the Captain would soon dispatch many of them with the push of a few buttons.

They finally reached the hatch for Engineering Control, and the Marine lifted his visor. His face was as red as it had been when Zax last saw it, but now it was from the pain and exertion of their journey rather than rage.

"I need a min, cadet."

Any additional time to think about the fate which lay on the other side of that hatch was the absolute last thing Zax needed, but he nodded at the sergeant nonetheless. He placed his ear upon the hatch and, for the first time since they had returned to Engineering, did not hear a cacophony of voices down below. There was plenty of discussion, but the volume level suggested the compartment held a similar number of occupants as when they last visited.

Zax closed his eyes and focused on deep breathing. He visualized dropping into compartment, spotting the Boss, and lifting his blaster to fire all in one smooth motion. He would not only take the shot, but he would also make the shot. Take the shot—make the shot—take the shot—make the shot. The silent mantra combined with the breathing exercises dropped Zax's pulse just low enough that he no longer felt as if his heart would burst from his chest. He never would have imagined spending the last moments of his life crouched in a maintenance tunnel with a mostly invisible Marine, but he found solace in the realization his impending sacrifice would have meaning.

He opened his eyes and saw the sergeant's color had returned to normal. A moment later the Marine turned to Zax and whispered.

"Are you ready?"

"Yes, Sergeant."

"Will you actually shoot this time?"

"Yes, Sergeant."

"Damn straight you will. Here's the plan. Open the hatch. I'm guessing they might start firing wildly, so be sure to stay back for a few secs. If they do shoot, eventually they'll stop. As soon as you have the chance, you should call out that you want to surrender. Jump down and be sure to get out of the way immediately because I will need to follow right behind before they have a chance to shut the hatch. If the Boss is in the compartment, cough twice and then give me a count of ten to prepare before you take your shot. I'll be ready to shoot at the same time as you. If he's not there, but eventually arrives, then use the same signal and countdown. Is all that clear?"

"Yes, Sergeant."

"Repeat it back to me."

"Hold back to avoid any fire when I open the hatch. When I get down, I need to move aside so you can follow behind me. When I see the Boss, cough twice and then count to ten before shooting."

"OK. Let's do this."

CHAPTER THIRTY-FOUR

Show your hands!

A cacophony of blaster fire echoed below the instant the hatch was cracked. Zax flung it open and held his body away from the opening to be sure that no stray fire reached him. There were short gaps in the shooting, but every time he went to open his mouth and speak someone would fire again and be joined by a number of others. Finally, someone below screamed for the shooting to halt and Zax hollered into the resulting silence.

"Please stop shooting. I want to surrender!"

"How many of you are up there?"

"Only me!"

"Show your hands! Slowly!"

Zax took one last deep breath of freedom and then slid his hands into view. The mini blaster ensconced in his right hand was hidden in plain sight thanks to its chameleon technology. There was no turning back.

"OK—drop down. You've got a half-dozen blasters pointed at you, so don't do anything stupid."

Zax maneuvered his body so his legs dangled through the hatch opening and then sprang down to the deck. He nailed the landing but made a show of sprawling forwards in a tangle of arms and legs while cursing theatrically. This not only allowed him to clear the space directly below the hatch for Bailee to land but also provided a distraction to ensure no one noticed the Marine's arrival. An invisible hand squeezed his calf for a moment, and Zax breathed a little easier with the knowledge he was not alone among the civilians.

He slowly stood and raised his hands into the air while glancing around the compartment. There were ten civilians present, but none of the Crew from Engineering. The Flight Boss was not in sight and neither was the small guy with the greasy black hair who had been in charge when the civilians commandeered the compartment. Zax recognized the civilian who appeared to be in charge now, but all of the others were new faces. A woman raced forwards with a chair which she used to reach and close the overhead hatch. Zax heard it automatically lock shut and knew his fate was sealed. He was going to die in the compartment with the only uncertainty being whether he managed to save the Ship in the process.

"Keep your hands up! Frisk him!"

The civilian who closed the hatch jumped down from the chair and searched Zax's body. He held his breath as she started at the cuffs of his sleeves and tightly squeezed every centimeter of both arms. Next, she tousled his hair as if there could be meaningful items hidden in his regulation short cut. The civilian's thorough search of his torso and lower body included a groping of his testicles that made him blush. When she reached his boots, she extracted the blade he had carried since taking it off the dead civilian earlier in the day. She tossed it to the civilian in charge who looked closely at the knife before he tucked it into his waistband.

Once the civilian completed her search, she backed away. The only parts of his body she had left untouched were his "empty" hands. Zax lowered them tentatively and no one stopped him. He breathed deeply to celebrate accomplishing the first critical step of his mission—he had smuggled both his own weapon and a fully-armed Marine into a heavily guarded stronghold of the civilian rebellion. The civilian in charge approached and spoke.

"What were you doing up there?"

Zax calibrated his tone for what he hoped was the right mix of emotions. He wanted to come across as being a young, scared kid without overdoing it too much. The civilian likely recognized him from earlier and probably was aware he had been on the loose for hours. If Zax tried to portray himself as being too helpless and afraid, the civilian might smell a rat.

"I got separated from the group I was with and couldn't find them. I was trying to get somewhere safe but kept running into groups of armed civilians. I finally decided to give up and hand myself over, but I didn't want to do it to some random group and risk them shooting me on sight."

The civilian grinned. "What makes you think we won't just shoot you?"

Zax gulped—primarily for show, but with more than a trace of concern. "Well...I was banking on the fact you didn't do it earlier when you first took over the compartment."

"Who were you running around with before you lost them?"

A story very close to truth struck Zax as being the best option. Any tales he might fabricate could easily bite him on the ass if Imair showed up and contradicted them. "The Marine sergeant and two other cadets who were here earlier. The sergeant is extremely injured, and we were trying to find some pain meds when a huge group of civilians showed up and we got separated. I tried to find them for a while but decided it was hopeless."

The civilian pondered Zax's story then spoke. "Let's see what Rege thinks. Get him in here."

One of the civilians near the hatch opened it and walked out. His steps echoed down the passageway until they were replaced with the babble of voices emanating from another compartment. Zax looked around as he waited. A giant pool of blood remained where the Crew bodies had been stacked earlier, but the corpses themselves were gone. The boxes Zax assumed contained explosives were still arrayed around the room, though they had been joined by a pile of similar ones which were stacked next to a closed hatch.

Two sets of footsteps eventually approached the open hatch and Zax looked back in that direction. He fought to maintain a neutral expression as Rege walked in—the man with the greasy hair who had done all of the speaking when the civilians took over the compartment. He carried a device in one hand which he lifted up as he smirked at Zax.

"I'm pleased to see you again, cadet. I'm dying to chat about what transpired after you left us earlier. First, though, I need to make sure you're really alone. Blasters ready everyone."

CHAPTER THIRTY-FIVE

Look who we have here.

Rege pressed a button on top of his device and there was bright flash accompanied by a loud bang. The air was filled with a fine mist and the civilians started to scan the room frantically. Zax was dumbfounded about what was happening until he noticed how the mist clung to the blaster in his hand and made its outline clearly visible. As nonchalantly as possible, he crossed his arms and hid the mini blaster in his armpit.

The good news for Zax was the civilians had their attention focused elsewhere and no one noticed his blaster before it was hidden. The bad news was that Sergeant Bailee's outline had become as clear as the weapon in Zax's hand. Two civilians grabbed the Marine's arms while two others sprinted forward with their blasters pointed at his head. Rege issued his orders.

"Look who we have here. Rip that helmet off and get his arms and legs tied up!"

A min later the mist which had outlined the Marine's ChamWare dissipated and his body once again faded away. His unhelmeted head remained visible, though, along with the bindings the civilians used to secure him. Zax looked down and pretended to itch his armpit and verified his blaster was again invisible. He dropped his arms into a more natural pose.

Rege strode towards the bound Marine and without saying a word punched him in the face. The sergeant swung his head back towards the civilian and defiantly spat a mouthful of blood onto the deck at his feet. Rege turned and walked towards Zax. He grabbed the chair the woman had used to close the hatch, spun it around, and sat with his arms perched on the back as he stared at Zax for a min. Finally, he spoke.

"Bring me the blade I heard this one was carrying."

The civilian who was holding it ran over and handed Rege the knife which had been taken from Zax. He unsheathed the blade and examined it closely. He focused on wiping a spot near the hilt with his sleeve as he spoke.

"You missed a little bit of blood here." Rege looked up and locked his gaze with Zax. "Tell me about how you came to be in possession of this knife."

Zax considered what to say. He was positive that he hadn't discussed their earlier escape within earshot of Imair, but he couldn't be absolutely certain that she hadn't overheard anything said by Kalare or Aleron. The potential for the civilian woman he once trusted to show up and contradict any lies prompted him to choose the truth once again. He sucked in a deep breath and launched into the story with as neutral a tone as he could manage.

"That huge civilian was about to leave us in a compartment when one of the other cadets said she needed to use the head. He gave her a bucket, and removed the bindings on her hands, but then she asked him to cut everyone else loose as well. She was worried one of us might need to use the bucket and she'd be force to help if we were still bound. The FTL jump occurred right then, and when I woke up I saw the his blaster had floated free and he was still unconscious. I tried to grab it, but he woke up. We were still wrestling over the weapon when gravity returned. He had almost strangled me to death when one of the other cadets stabbed him in order to save me."

"Which of the other two cadets actually killed him?"

Zax flashed back to Kalare holding the bloody knife over the dead civilian's body. His instinct to protect his friend at all costs kicked in and overrode the previous decision to share the truth with Rege. He held his eyes steady with the civilian's and answered his question without a moment's hesitation.

"I had blacked out by the end, and the knife was just sitting on the deck when I came to. I didn't care who did it and didn't bother to ask since I was just grateful to be alive."

Rege turned his gaze to the knife as he twirled it over and over in his hand. His expression was oddly wistful until he finally sighed and then spoke. "I've always loved this knife. I remember how jealous I was when my father gave it to my brother. We were young and the old man had pitted us against each other in another one of his crazy contests. That was the last time I lost to him, but there was never another prize I wanted as much as I had wanted this knife. I tried and tried to get my brother to swap it for something else— even stuff that was way more valuable—but he never budged. Once he realized how much I wanted it, I think he decided to keep it simply as payback for losing to me so much. It positively killed him that I was so much smaller than he was and yet managed to win all the time."

Zax was dismayed to learn the civilian who Kalare had stabbed was actually Rege's brother. They barely seemed like they had come from the same species much less the same parents. Zax became increasingly anxious about how Rege might react to his role in the giant's death and decided his only option was to try to justify it to the civilian.

"I'm sorry to hear he was your brother, but what were those other cadets supposed to do—let him kill me? We were only in that damn situation because the two of you showed up here with the rest of your friends and started murdering people for no reason."

Rege stared at Zax for a few beats until a grin broke out on his face.

"No reason? That's funny, cadet, painfully funny. Let me share a story and maybe you'll decide to rethink that assessment."

Rege stood up from the chair and paced back and forth around Zax as he calmly spoke.

"I was saying before how I always wanted this knife, but it was just as well my brother held on to it. I don't know what would have happened otherwise the day my father snapped. You see—our little sister got real sick. Dene was always my father's favorite. Our mother died during her birth and I guess that leaves a man with two choices. He can blame and shun the baby or love on it like crazy as the last echo of the woman he lost. My father chose the latter and doted on Dene. The two of us boys were forced to fight for scraps while she always got the best of whatever meager rations he scraped together. Sometimes I hated her for it, but usually understood it wasn't her fault. She was a good kid.

"So Dene gets sick and my father goes for meds. She didn't need anything exotic, just basic antivirals. There were shortages at the time, so the medics wouldn't give him anything. They told him they needed to save it all for the Crew. He tried everything he could to score some from unofficial sources, but everyone demanded far more in return than he had to give. I watched him cradle Dene as she burned up from the fever. She had a bunch of intense seizures at the end. Real gruesome stuff to watch.

"She finally stopped seizing and went still and my father wailed. I put my hand on his shoulder to try and comfort him, and he spun around looking crazy. Something must have broken inside him after watching both his wife and then his little girl die in his arms. He was looking right at me, but his eyes were empty.

"He threw me around the compartment and pounded me nearly senseless. My brother heard the commotion and somehow got him off me. The old man wasn't done though and went after him too. He had beaten me so badly I could barely lift my head off the deck, so all I could do was watch as they grappled. Finally, my father backed away and I saw this knife sticking out of his chest. The pain must have shocked him into realizing what he had done. He looked over and told me he was sorry before he keeled over dead."

Rege stopped pacing and instead moved towards Zax with the knife extended. Zax tensed but didn't flinch as the blade came within milimeters of his left eye and the civilian spoke again.

"So that's what pushed my brother and I to get involved with the group who planned all of this. Some bureaucrat decided that keeping meds available *just in case* a member of the Crew needed them was a better use of resources than saving my sister who was sick *at that very moment* and could have been easily saved. Does that bureaucrat's decision seem reasonable to you, cadet?"

Zax was at a loss for words. A million potential replies came to mind, but none seemed more likely than the others to prevent the furious civilian from driving the blade into his skull. He was about to voice one when Sergeant Bailee spoke instead.

"It seems perfectly reasonable to me. Your sister died, but what's more important—saving one little girl or making sure the Ship has whatever we need to treat the fighter pilots who protect us from aliens? And what about the Marines who ensure safe planets for our colonists. Isn't it important to make sure the Ship has the drugs necessary to keep them healthy? Do you consider either of those factors when you decide what's reasonable, or can you not see past your sister to look at the big picture? The universe is trying to kill all of us as fast as it possibly can. Better we lose one girl than have the Mission fail. Right?"

Rege spun around to face the Marine and the two locked glares. Zax held his breath and feared for what would happen next—especially the possibility of the civilian pulling out the collar controller for some torture. Rege charged towards Bailee but halted when another civilian ran up and called out.

"Rege—someone's calling in about a Marine and a couple of cadets they've captured. They want to know what to do with them."

CHAPTER THIRTY-SIX

There's nothing you can do, Zax!

It took all of Zax's self-control to remain impassive at the civilian's words. He held his breath as the man approached and handed over some sort of wireless communicator.

"Report!" barked Rege into the device.

"We found a Marine and two cadets trying to reach the garrison near us. The Marine got hurt in the firefight and the two cadets surrendered. We weren't sure what to do with the prisoners after we heard things are going to be over soon."

Rege turned and stared at Zax while he posed a question to the person on the other end of the comm. "What are the names on their uniforms?"

"The Marine is only wearing an undershirt which does not have a name. The male cadet is wearing an Engineering uniform and the name on it is Aleron. The female cadet is wearing a Flight uniform and the name reads Kalare."

As hard as he tried to prevent it, Zax's body flinched ever so slightly at the mention of Kalare's name. Rege grinned when he observed the involuntary movement.

"Hold for orders." Rege lowered the communicator and moved in closer to Zax. "Thank you for just confirming those are your friends who we've captured. We're about to take over the Ship for good, and we've been given orders to take prisoners rather than kill any more Crew to build goodwill. I'm very tight with our leader, though, and I'm confident she'll be OK with making an exception for the person who killed my brother. Since you've already told me you don't know who actually stabbed him, I guess I'll be forced to have our people execute both cadets."

Zax's emotions roiled at the outcome of his earlier lie. In trying to protect Kalare, he had actually made it impossible to save her. Zax didn't know if he would have been capable of issuing Aleron a death sentence by falsely identifying him as the killer of Rege's brother, but in hindsight he wished he had left that option open. Instead, the untruth had only served to paint him into a corner.

Rege brandished the knife once more as he leaned in closer to Zax. "Or maybe I should have them brought here. I can take their two lives with the same blade that took two lives from my family. Seems like that would be nice symmetry, don't you think? You say you blacked out and didn't get to see my brother die, so we can make sure you're conscious for these two deaths. You really should get to witness what happens when a knife is jammed in to the back of someone's neck. See how the spark of a life gets extinguished with a simple twist of the blade. Watch how the blood pools on the deck while the body cools and stiffens. What do you think, cadet, does that sound like a good plan?"

Every muscle in Zax's body tensed. None more so than those in the hand which grasped the invisible mini blaster. He exulted in the thought of how easy it would be to save Kalare by simply killing the civilian before he could exact his revenge upon her. Zax was on the verge of lifting his arm to take the shot when Sergeant Bailee called out.

"There's nothing you can do, Zax!"

Anger clouded Rege's face as he turned and closed the remaining distance between him and the Marine with the blade in his outstretched arm. The sergeant held the civilian's furious gaze without flinching in the face of impending death. At the last second, Rege flipped the blade so that he held it by the upper portion of the hilt. He smashed the butt of the handle into Bailee's temple with punishing force. The Marine crashed to the deck unconscious.

Zax was now entirely on his own with the civilians, but the sergeant's words echoed in his mind. The Marine knew there was something Zax *could* do in the situation. He *could* use his hidden weapon to kill Rege before the civilian issued any further orders and hopefully save Kalare in the process. What the Marine must have been trying to tell Zax was that there was nothing he *should* do. The irony was not lost on Zax as he unpacked Bailee's directive. He was supposed to not shoot an insurgent and spare two Crew because he actually needed to save it for killing a different Crew member.

Rege strutted back towards Zax. "Where were we? Oh yes, I was asking you whether you wanted to have your friends brought here so you can see what it looks like when someone dies by the blade. How does that sound?"

The pull weight of the blaster's trigger pushed back against the muscles of Zax's finger. His outward appearance remained neutral while his inner dialog was as riled as the most storm swept planet. He attempted to calm himself by envisioning how the one motion of raising his arm and firing the blaster would kill Rege and end the threat on Kalare's life. The civilians had been told to spare their Crew prisoners, and Zax fought to convince himself that would remain the default action of the people on the other end of the communicator who held her.

Some part of Zax knew there was something wrong with that logic, however, and kept his arm plastered to his side. Yes, he could dream that removing Rege from the equation would prevent the civilians from killing Kalare, but he had no way of guaranteeing that outcome. Perhaps, he worried, they would still kill her simply out of spite.

A more likely scenario surfaced from the maelstrom of his thoughts. He believed that killing Rege would most likely protect Kalare from the immediate threat, but concluded her salvation would be short-lived. She, along with almost everyone else on board, was slated to die within mins once the Captain vented the Ship and ended the revolution. The only thing that could stop that outcome was if the civilians tortured the Boss so effectively he cracked quickly and provided them access to the FTL engine. They would then hold its possible destruction as the ultimate chip in the negotiations and force a halt to the Captain's plans. Kalare wouldn't get vented into space, but she would be stuck on a Ship controlled by civilians. If Rege exemplified the grudges and hatreds that underpinned the civilians' actions, there was a torturous existence awaiting the Crew under their command.

Zax released his finger from the trigger in resignation. There was no good outcome available for Kalare. The only thing which made sense was keeping the existence of his weapon secret and holding out hope it would be used to accomplish his original mission. It was impossible to guarantee his friend's safety, but at least he could offer his own life alongside hers in an effort to save the Ship and its Mission from the civilians. In a final act of defiance, he turned away from Rege so he would not be tempted to change his mind by the man's self-satisfied facial expression.

"Don't you turn your back on me, boy!"

Zax heard the knife clatter to the deck and the civilian's pounding footfalls approach as he roared his disapproval. A fist crashed into Zax's right kidney and he fell forward to the deck on his hands and knees. He gasped, not from the searing pain, but from the realization he nearly lost his grip on the precious blaster. He curled into a ball and cradled the invisible weapon close to his body. He glared up at the civilian as he fantasized about taking two shots in quick succession—one to kill the Boss and save the Ship from civilian control and a second which would extinguish Rege's miserable life. He sought solace in the desperate hope the Boss might appear before Kalare could be delivered to Rege. That dream was quickly dashed as the civilian looked down at the screen of his communicator and spoke.

"Look at how late it's gotten. You and your Marine friend have made me waste a lot of time, cadet, right when things are about to get really interesting around here. Now I'm not going to be able to take care of those other two myself." He keyed the communicator. "Kill the two cadets. Make sure it's painful. Rege out."

CHAPTER THIRTY-SEVEN

She's in for the surprise of her life.

Zax choked back an anguished scream. He refused to give the civilian the satisfaction of seeing the pain he had caused. Zax closed his eyes and fought to calm down. All he could envision was the suffering being visited upon Kalare. His friend, his dear, dear friend, had just heard her death sentence announced and was likely experiencing its excruciating delivery. Zax had lost the chance to save her but silently vowed to avenge her. If the civilian was still in the compartment when the Boss appeared, Rege would also be dead before the Omega's lifeless body hit the deck.

"What the hell's going on in here, Rege? I told you I didn't want any more violence!"

Zax recognized the voice. He opened his eyes and looked at the hatch to see Imair enter the compartment. He noticed all of the civilians stand straighter—almost as if they were Crew snapping to attention in the presence of an Omega. She smiled benevolently at him.

"Hello, Zax. I'm certainly not surprised you managed to find your way here." She glanced at Sergeant's Bailee's unconscious form. "I had a feeling we had a shadow in ChamWare when I was with you earlier. It makes perfect sense for the sergeant to show up and try to interfere with my plans, and he'd need your navigating skills and tunnel access to make that happen. We never had an opportunity to test out that mist device before today, but I know my engineers will be thrilled to learn it worked as intended."

Zax struggled to reconcile what he was seeing and hearing. His confusion must have been apparent because Imair grinned even more broadly.

"I can see you're puzzled, Zax. I'll be happy to explain and answer your questions in a moment, but I need to take care of a couple items first. Rege—hand me that communicator."

Imair took the comm unit proffered by Rege and fiddled with its controls for a moment. She started to speak and Zax was astounded to hear her words emanate from the vid screens in the room. It wasn't her actual voice, but rather the disguised one he had heard when the civilians first took over the Engineering compartment. Zax had indeed recognized the speaker when he listened earlier because it was someone he had heard repeatedly for the past year.

"Greetings, everyone. It's been a while since you last heard from either me or the Captain. My apologies. We thought at the time we had an agreement in hand which would allow us to end these hostilities, and I had hoped to report more progress by now. Unfortunately, final resolution has taken longer than planned. Regardless, I'm now confident we'll be able to end all of this unpleasantness *one way or the other* in a very short period of time. Please expect to hear back from me soon."

Imair looked down at the communicator and manipulated its controls once again. The Captain appeared on one of the vidscreens. Since it was only one screen and not all of them, Zax assumed it was a private channel and not being broadcast to the entire Ship. The Captain looked up and frustration filled her voice as she spoke.

"What exactly was that announcement supposed to mean?"

Imair grinned as she replied, even though it appeared to only be an audio channel on her end and her visage was not being transmitted.

"I'm not sure what you could be upset about, Captain. If anything, we should be the ones annoyed by all of your delays. We are almost halfway to your 240 min deadline, and you have not yet delivered on some of my demands we had agreed to. For instance, why haven't the environmental controls been transferred to Engineering yet?"

Hearing Imair say it was nearly 120 mins since her last announcement made Zax remember the Captain was in her final preparations to vent the Ship. He could see the Crew moving frantically all around the bridge behind her on the screen and tried to imagine what it would be like to kill nearly ten million people with the push of a button. Zax closely watched the Captain's expression and was duly impressed at how she gave away nothing. She held her hands out in a pleading gesture.

"Look around me—we're doing our best. I've got everyone scrambling, but there was so much damage from the bombs and it's causing us problems. I'm confident we'll have some good news to report in just a few more mins."

Zax thought he caught a glint in the Captain's eyes with her last sentence. Imair's tone and expression did not change as she responded.

"Regardless, we'll have some new developments on this end as well in that timeframe. I encourage you to remember who's in charge right now, Captain. Our control is about to become even more solidified, and I would hate to see you break your word and not honor your earlier commitments. There will be severe consequences for noncompliance."

Imair delivered her last words with grave sincerity and cut the connection. She turned to Zax.

"That woman thinks I'm an idiot. She's in for the surprise of her life. You must have a million questions for me, Zax, but I only have a couple of mins available before I need to finalize our takeover. Ask your most pressing one first."

Zax actually had only one thought at that moment, and he locked eyes with Imair. "How could you kill Nolly?"

A dark cloud passed over Imair's face, but her countenance soon shifted back to her typical neutral expression.

"Really, Zax? I give you an opportunity to ask me *anything,* and that's the best you can come up with? I'm disappointed in you. I'm sorry to hear he died as that was not my intent. It was critical that I distract you folks for a while after I took off with the Boss. I only wanted to hurt him, but I'm not much of a marksman and felt with only one shot I needed to aim near center mass. I regret taking the life of a child, but I believe even he would agree it was a small price to pay in order to preserve the future for untold billions of civilians by putting an end to this Ship's insane Mission.

"You came close to really screwing up our plans, Zax. Freeing the Boss and then helping to kill the Chief Engineer took away our best chances of capturing the Ship. Thankfully your group did exactly what I anticipated and went to Waste Management. The real value of all your strict Crew training, as far as I'm concerned, is that it leads all of you to act very predictably. I took a big chance by putting myself at risk to track you down and infiltrate your little traveling party, but I did so with the confidence I was almost surely guaranteed to succeed."

Imair looked over at the open hatch in response to the sound of a group approaching and smiled. "Rege—help the cadet to his feet and grab a blaster. I want to bring him along with us to the FTL compartment so he can witness first-hand the end of the Crew's command of this Ship."

Zax used his empty hand to brush away Rege's assistance and followed Imair's gaze as he got to his feet. His heart began to pound furiously as he watched the Flight Boss enter the compartment.

CHAPTER THIRTY-EIGHT

What have you done?

Zax's body tensed as he surveyed the situation. A half dozen civilians poured into the compartment alongside the Boss, and the man calmly spoke with one who walked beside him. The Omega looked exactly the same as he had when Zax last saw him. He expected the civilians to have been torturing the officer this entire time and was perplexed when the man did not appear to have been abused the way the Chief Engineer had earlier in the day. He could not in a million years imagine what might have caused the Boss to break faster than anyone would have anticipated, but the civilians must have done something truly dreadful if Imair was so confident she was about to gain access to the FTL.

There would be no hesitation this time. Kalare's murder had cemented Zax's resolve to complete the mission Sergeant Bailee had assigned. His finger tightened on the trigger. He casually turned so his right arm would be pointed directly at the Boss when he lifted the blaster for his shot. As he did so, he made a mental note of Rege's position. The civilian was standing less than a meter away on Zax's right side. He was laughing having just awkwardly caught a blaster by the barrel which someone tossed to him. Zax would have to move quickly if we was going to get off a second shot and kill the civilian, but he felt confident in his abilities.

Zax stared at the Boss and casually lifted his arm to fire the kill shot. Time felt like it slowed painfully, but Zax feared attracting unwanted attention if he moved too quickly. The Omega stopped speaking with the woman next to him, and his eyes swept the compartment as he entered. His gaze paused for a moment and he raised his eyebrows slightly when he saw Sergeant Bailee's body, clad mostly in ChamWare, lying unconscious on the deck. The Boss's head continued to turn and his eyes went wide as they met Zax's.

"The cadet has a weapon!"

The Boss's words echoed through the compartment as the officer hunched down in an effort to shield himself. Zax was confused as to why the man would endanger an outcome he had to expect and should actually desire, but in the end it didn't matter.

By ducking the Boss only hastened his demise as the movement placed his head into the same plane as Zax's arm. He pulled the trigger for the kill shot.

Zax's leg erupted in blinding pain. The limb had shattered from the force of Rege wielding his blaster like a club and smashing the weapon's stock against it. The impact threw off Zax's aim by a few millimeters just as the trigger fully engaged. His shot bounced harmlessly off a bulkhead as Zax crashed to the deck once again. He finally lost his grip on the blaster which became visible as it skittered away.

Imair berated the civilians before the blaster shot had even stopped reverberating.

"How in the hell did everyone manage to miss he was carrying a blaster? Who frisked him?"

Rege moved to pick up the blaster and smiled as it went invisible in his hand. He held it up for everyone to see.

"This is how we missed it. Looks like the Marines have some tricks we weren't aware of."

Imair shook her head ruefully as she held out her hand for the weapon. Rege handed it over and she tucked it into the waistband of her pants in the small of her back. She spoke quietly with him while the activity level in the compartment increased markedly. A group of civilians approached the closed hatch and started to pick up the crates of explosives which were stacked there. One held it open as the others carried the boxes into the compartment beyond.

Zax laid on the deck and silently wept. Not from the agony of his leg, but from shame. He had failed. In everything. Kalare was dead and the Boss was alive. His friend was gone and soon all hope for the Ship would be as well. He felt a hand on his shoulder and looked up into the eyes of the Flight Boss.

"What have you done?" Zax hissed through his tears.

"I'm sorry, Zax," the Omega whispered. "I don't expect you to understand. I couldn't let you kill me, though I respect you immensely for trying. I hope you'll some day look back and see why this was all for the best. You've accomplished your duty today, Zax, better than I ever would've dreamed."

Zax was overwhelmed with an urge to spit in the officer's face. The man was allowing the civilians to win and appeared to be doing so without any semblance of a fight. Why had Zax sacrificed so much to try to save the Ship and protect the Crew if its second highest ranking officer was willing to just up and quit? Imair appeared over the Omega's shoulder and pulled the man up by the arm before Zax could act on his disgust.

"Come on, *Boss*. Time to deliver my prize like you promised. Let's go visit the FTL."

The officer pushed her hand away brusquely. "I'm not going anywhere without the cadet."

Imair looked at Zax's tear-streaked face and his twisted leg. "He doesn't much seem like he can manage to go anywhere. Leave him be and I promise no one will harm him. The sooner we get this over with, the sooner we can get him proper medical attention."

The Boss, ignoring Imair's directive, knelt down and scooped Zax into his arms. Zax felt wildly conflicted. The Boss was willing to throw all of their fates to the mercy of these horrific civilians, but for some reason he still attempted to protect Zax. His body initially recoiled at the man's touch, but he fought to calm himself and eventually settled into the Omega's arms.

Imair frowned. "Fine. Have it your way, but he better not disrupt things again or he'll have more to worry about than a busted leg."

CHAPTER THIRTY-NINE

Please open the hatch.

The Boss carried Zax and followed Imair to the hatch. She held it open as they passed into the FTL anteroom. It was a nondescript compartment, though Zax knew it was adjacent to the most heavily armored space in the Ship and multiple meters of exotic alloys stood between him and the engine. The FTL device itself was benign, but the Ship's designers were well aware of its strategic value as a target. The armor was intended to protect it from all enemies both alien and Shipbound. Only the Ship's total annihilation would penetrate all of its layers of protection. That, Zax rued, or one of the Omegas with access deciding to hand it over without so much as a whimper.

Once the Boss provided his biometrics to the reader which controlled the final hatch, it would open and the civilian scum would pour in and rig their explosives around the engine. The Captain would never risk the destruction of the FTL and would be forced to acquiesce to the civilians' demands. The distances involved in interstellar travel were so vast, only the engine's ability to instantly jump from one star system to another allowed the Ship to move far enough fast enough that humanity could survive. Their food and energy reserves would be depleted long before the Ship reached another system at sublight velocity.

Imair continued towards the interior hatch which led to the FTL, but the Boss halted. She realized he was no longer behind her, turned, and snapped.

"You're the one who told me we needed to rush. Get moving!"

The Boss looked around the compartment and gestured towards its many occupants. "Not until you get all of them out of here. There will be plenty of time for your team to load in the explosives later. When I speak with the Captain, I don't want anyone present except you and the boy."

Imair stormed back to the Boss and forced her face as close to his as she could without crushing Zax between them in the officer's arms. "What makes you think you're in a position where I should give a damn about what you want? How about I send someone to grab the controller and we can have a little fun with your collar?"

Zax held his breath in suspense for nearly a min as Imair glared at the Boss and the man stared impassively back at her. The civilian finally gasped in surprise when the lighting in the compartment switched to amber and a loud klaxon wailed. She swiveled her head all around trying to identify the threat. The Boss grinned.

"*That* is why you should give a damn about what I want. The Captain has disabled the life support systems throughout the Ship. The alarm here and in Engineering Control is only informational because we're covered by an emergency system and will be fine, but oxygen replenishment is about to cease almost everywhere else. You don't have to worry about any of your people running out of air, though, because the Captain is also preparing to vent the entire Ship and send all ten million of them into space. Assuming she continues to follow the procedures to the letter, it will all be over in less than three hundred secs. You'll eventually figure out how to force me to open that hatch and get you into the FTL, but I'm beyond confident that I can hold out against any torture for at least that long."

Imair paused for a moment, but then stepped back and bellowed over the combined din of the alarms and the civilians' activity. "Clear the compartment! Everything's going according to plan, but I need *everyone* to leave. Now!"

The civilians initially froze from indecision, but Imair's final exclamation sent them scurrying out of the compartment. Rege herded everyone out and then shut the hatch as he was the last to leave. The Boss gently placed Zax down on the deck and held out his hand to Imair. The civilian handed him the communicator and stepped back. The Omega fiddled with the controls for a moment, and then the Captain's image appeared on the vidscreen mounted on the wall. Zax could see the Boss was broadcasting his own image as well. The Captain recognized her fellow Omega and smiled.

"I didn't expect to see you right now, Boss. You must be aware of what I'm doing, so I hope you can understand this really isn't a great time for a chat."

"My apologies, ma'am, but that's entirely why I'm calling. I need you to put a halt to your plans and stand down."

The Captain appeared confused for a moment but then grinned. "That's a good one, Boss. I'd almost think you were trying to make a joke if I didn't know you so well. I really do need to get back to business right now."

"Ma'am—I regret to inform you that Alpha has invoked Order Sixty-Six, and as the second highest ranking officer I've concurred. You're being relieved of your rank effective immediately."

The Captain's mouth dropped in response to the Boss's statement. She paused for a moment until she regrouped.

"Where are you right now, Boss?"

"I'm in the FTL anteroom, ma'am. The civilians will be entering the engine compartment momentarily to rig it with explosives. I've negotiated with their leader and Alpha to craft a solution which will end this uprising without any further loss of life. I will retain my position and command of the Crew, albeit under the oversight of our new civilian President. The civilians will use their ability to destroy the FTL engine to guarantee Crew compliance going forwards. You'll rescind the order to vent the Ship, reengage all life support, and return to your quarters immediately."

Zax could not believe his ears, but the rationale behind the Boss's actions had become crystal clear. He not only saved his own skin by allowing the civilians to enter the FTL compartment and take the device hostage but also maintained his position of power even with the transition to civilian control.

The Captain grimaced. "I always figured you had something like this in you, but Alpha insisted I support your rise to command every step of the way. What happens if I refuse and press this button here to commence the venting?"

"Frankly, ma'am, the same thing that happens if you agree. In either case, you're going out an airlock. The difference is that if you don't cooperate, it will only happen after you've endured ghastly retribution. I urge you to do the honorable thing. Halt your orders. Step aside. Our time has passed, ma'am.

We need to give the civilians a chance to run the show now."

The Captain cracked a wry smile. "I honestly have a hard time disagreeing with your sentiment, Boss, but it seems strange that you've somehow managed to finagle things so you're still effectively in charge."

"Ma'am, this is not an outcome I sought. I've spent the day doing everything I could to block the civilians from achieving their goals. Once I was captured, it became clear to Alpha this was the best remaining outcome. I urge you to stand down, ma'am. We lost. They won. The best thing you can do now is accept your own death and with it spare the lives of ten million innocents."

The Captain looked pensive for a moment before she spoke. "I will do it on one condition, Boss. I want you to be the one pressing the button which sends me out the airlock. No coup is rightfully complete until the new leader is baptized with the blood of the old."

The Boss looked to Imair for her approval. The civilian had watched the back and forth with intense interest and smiled when the Captain bitterly spat out her final words. She nodded to the Boss, and he repeated the gesture to the Captain. The video connection with the bridge went dead and a few secs later the klaxon silenced and the lights returned to normal.

"Well done, Boss," Imair said. "I can see we're going to work very well together moving forward. I must say, though, how surprising it is to learn the depths of the Captain's mistrust of you. It's clear I need to keep an eye on you, even more so than would be obvious given the way in which we've been thrust together. Regardless, it's time for you to deliver the last part of our deal. Please open the hatch."

The Boss didn't look at Imair but approached the hatch in response. As he did so, a small control panel lit up blinking red and he placed his hand upon it. After a moment, the panel flashed yellow and the Boss spoke, "Alpha-1178-Zeta-07291." With the access code completing the process, the panel glowed green and the hatch began to slide aside. What had appeared to be a normal hatch from the outside slowly cracked open and revealed itself to be unimaginably thick.

The Boss returned to Zax and scooped him up once again. The man's expression was one of remorse initially, but he switched to a tight smile as he spoke to Zax.

"Come on, cadet. We might as well get you a glimpse of the FTL engine as long as we're here. Who knows how long it will be before it gets destroyed."

The hatch had completed its ponderous opening process by the time they approached it. The Boss stepped into the compartment, and Zax was underwhelmed as he looked around. It was even more boring in appearance than the anteroom which preceded it. The Boss carried him near the device which stood alone in the middle of the room. Zax's breath was taken away as he viewed the FTL engine up close.

It was a sphere which measured a meter in diameter and from afar appeared to be dark and lifeless. Zax's first glance had suggested it was of uniform color and density, but a closer inspection revealed it shimmered with twinkling lights. The more Zax focused, the more he saw the lights actually appeared to be stars, constellations, and nebulae. It was almost as if someone had captured a galaxy within that sphere, and Zax was thoroughly mesmerized as he stared deeper and deeper into the device.

Zax reverie was broken when he felt the Boss jostled. The civilians had begun to stream in. The Boss turned to exit the compartment, but he crashed into a civilian as he did so and lost his balance. They both fell to the deck and their combined mass came down on Zax's shattered leg. The pain was so intense that he lost consciousness, but not before he made note of the gleeful expressions on the faces of the civilians as they carried in their crates. Crates filled with explosives which guaranteed their control of every decision which would be made on the Ship going forwards.

CHAPTER FORTY

I'm making good on that promise.

"Cadet—it's time to wake up." Zax ignored the male voice. There was a dull ache from nearly his entire body, with the exception being his right leg where the pain was more intense. He had vague memories of civilians and blasters and klaxons, but thinking about any of that seemed like it could wait until he had slept for a few more days. Zax scrunched his eyes tight and wished he could somehow do the same to his ears. He felt a transdermal injector against his arm and a moment later his eyes opened with a start. Whatever drug he had been given took effect and sent him into instant arousal.

A medic smiled down at Zax—the same man who had cared for him a year ago when he came back from the alien planet and was subsequently Plugged

In. "Welcome back to the land of the living, cadet. You've been out for thirty-six hours and only eight of those can be attributed to the effects of the anesthesia we used. You've already been hit with five hundred demerits for oversleeping, and I figured that was enough. Plus, someone really wants to speak with you."

The medic left the compartment and Zax took inventory of his condition. His right leg was encased in an aerogel cast, and he thought back to how it had been broken. The pain he felt must be the aftereffects of the bone being knit back together. He found himself grateful for the idea of being stuck in the medbay for a little while longer as it meant he could avoid returning to duty.

Duty. Zax wondered what exactly his duty even was any longer. The civilians had captured the Ship. Correction—the Boss had let the civilians capture the Ship. Was Zax supposed to report back to Waste Systems once he was healthy as if nothing had happened? The hatch opened and Sergeant Bailee entered.

"How're you feeling, cadet?" The gruff Marine continued without waiting for any reply. "I've heard about what went down after I got knocked out and wanted to commend you. I know how badly you wanted to shoot that civilian and protect Kalare, but you did the right thing by not doing so. I also wanted to assure you that no one blames you for missing your shot and not killing the Boss. After all, it's not like you're a Marine or anything. Maybe I'll get a chance to beat some more training into you, and we'll make a proper marksman of you yet."

The sergeant turned and walked out without a further word. Zax was flooded with emotion. On one hand, he was dumbfounded by the Marine's words. Why had he made any mention of Zax getting "blamed" for missing that shot? It was impossible for anyone to think Zax could have done anything better. The Boss would surely be dead and the Captain would have successfully ended the uprising by venting the Ship if the Omega had not revealed the presence of Zax's blaster at the very last moment.

The more dominant emotion was grief at the memory of Kalare being killed by the civilians when he could have shot Rege and given her at least a temporary reprieve. He chose his mission to save the Ship over protecting his friend, only to see that mission fail due to the actions of its intended target. He closed his eyes and fought back his grief. The hatch started to open again, and Zax rolled over to face away from it. He desperately hoped the medic would take the hint and come back later.

After a few secs of silence, a chair was pulled up next to the bed and someone sat down. His curiosity finally got the better of him, so Zax rolled over and came face to face with the Boss. The man smiled around a cigar which was once again clamped between his teeth. As was often the case, Zax didn't think the expression quite reached all the way to the Omega's eyes.

"Greetings, Zax. How do you feel?"

A million different potential responses flooded Zax's mind. The most prominent was jumping out of bed and killing the man with his bare hands. That didn't seem feasible given the state of his leg, so Zax simply remained silent and stared blankly at the officer. The man's expression tightened slightly, but he maintained the smile.

"No need to say anything. I understand you're probably still feeling groggy from being unconscious for so long. Not to mention whatever pain meds they have you on. It's been a pretty crazy day and a half around here while you've been recovering, though you probably could have guessed that. I don't have too much time because I've got a meeting with the President, but I asked them to notify me as soon as you were awake so I could come and formally thank you for everything you did.

"Before we left Waste Systems on our way to the Marine garrison, I had promised you would be rewarded if you kept me out of the hands of the civilians. I'm making good on that promise. We know things didn't quite go according to plan, but there's no way you should be held responsible for the final outcome."

The Omega paused for a deep breath and continued. "I will be awarding you 50,000 credits. I'd like you back in the Threat chair once we finish getting Flight Ops restored, and I've arranged for you to receive a spot in the Pilot Academy. Finally, I'm offering once again to be your mentor. I believe you have the capacity for true greatness, and I want to do everything I can to be sure you achieve your potential. Hell, you might even get to be Captain some day if we ever actually have one again. What do you say, cadet?"

Zax was speechless, but his rage had been displaced by absolute shock. He quickly did the math and concluded that 50,000 credits would move him all the way to the very top of the Leaderboard. Not only would he be back working in Flight Ops, but he'd also be back on the path to achieving his lifelong dream of being a pilot. It was everything he had fantasized about for the past long year of working in that hellhole Waste Systems. Except—

"I hope you can understand my confusion, sir. I've been sitting here worrying about how I didn't accomplish what I was told was critical to save the Ship. In fact, Sergeant Bailee was just in here a few mins ago to reassure me that no one blamed me for missing the shot and not killing you like I was supposed to. It seemed odd, though, how he thought I would feel responsible given how the outcome of that shot wasn't the least bit my fault. It was yours."

The smile faded from the man's face. He appraised Zax for a few secs before speaking.

"I told you at the time, Zax, that I didn't expect you to understand my actions and that's still true. I did what I did with the firm conviction I chose the best option for the Ship out of what was available. For what it's worth, the civilians have been true to their word and everything is getting back to normal. Accept what I'm offering. Let me teach you the lessons of true leadership and I promise that someday you'll look back on all of this and it will make perfect sense."

For the second time in a year, Zax found himself at a turning point in his life which entirely hinged on how he responded to the Omega. Was he be capable of setting aside all of his concerns and doubts about the Boss?

Was the man responsible for Mikedo's death and did he then try to have Zax and Kalare killed as well, or had that all been a horrible coincidence? Kalare was convinced the Boss was innocent, but she'd never provided an explanation sufficient to assuage Zax's concerns. And what about how the Omega effectively handed control over to the civilians without a struggle? He claimed that Alpha initiated the order and he only agreed out of his duty to protect the Ship, but Zax had a hard time looking past yet another coincidence where the Ship's interests also happened to align perfectly with what was best for the Boss. Did Zax really want to ally himself with someone who might ultimately prove to be a murderous schemer, someone prepared to do anything to retain his power?

Last year Zax chose to stand by his convictions and defied the Boss. He exposed the existence of the human fighter and revealed how Mikedo was most likely murdered in an attempt to cover it up. What had sacrificing his career back then achieved? It obviously triggered massive changes on board the Ship, but it didn't cause much impact on the Boss himself. He just chugged along in power while Zax wasted a year of his life in Waste Systems. Sure the civilians had taken over, but hadn't the Flight Boss really just traded one boss for another? If anything, his power had only increased since he was now effectively in charge of the Crew and just dealing with civilian "oversight" for the big decisions.

Why should Zax turn down the man's offer again? He had already suffered for a year and achieved nothing. He deserved to get his career back on the track it was before. If anything, getting close with the Omega again might allow Zax to uncover evidence of the man's guilt which Kalare missed during her time with him. Zax finally nodded his acceptance.

The Boss smiled again. "Good decision, Zax. I understand you'll be getting out of here tomorrow morning. Report to my conference room after breakfast, and we'll talk about what will come next."

The Omega left and Zax closed his eyes to obsess about that very same thing—what *will* come next?

CHAPTER FORTY-ONE

Not this all over again...

The next morning Zax skipped the opportunity for a final meal in bed in favor of getting out of medbay and checking out what was happening around the Ship in the wake of the civilian revolution. His leg felt weak and he still required a few days' worth of physical therapy, but, for the most part, his body had recovered from the shock. His mind, however, was a different story. Particularly whenever he allowed his thoughts to slip back to Kalare.

His first destination was his berth for a new uniform. He had been discharged from medbay into the same uniform he was wearing when they brought him in, and it still reeked of Waste Systems. Zax was tempted to burn it altogether and suffer the huge slug of demerits for wanton destruction of resources, but he decided otherwise once he walked in and saw his name listed at the very top of the Leaderboard display in the Theta berth. He wasn't going to do anything that would throw any of those hard-earned points away. At least, not right away.

Zax's breath caught when he noticed Kalare's name a few slots below his. He breathed deeply for a full min to keep his emotions in check. Damn administrators. Leaderboard scores were always accurate since they were updated automatically in real time, but there was often a delay in removing names from the Leaderboard when Crew were Culled. Or in Kalare's case, murdered by civilians.

The Theta berth was empty, but otherwise looked the same as when he had left to share his completed sim with Kalare over breakfast just a few days earlier. Everything he had seen along the way, in fact, looked exactly the same. Zax expected armed rebels to be roaming the passageways but had not seen a single civilian. The only weapon was carried by a Marine who looked like he was heading to guard duty somewhere.

Zax stripped out of his uniform and took a shower which was regulation in both length and temperature. He got dressed and walked quickly to the mess hall to grab breakfast before his scheduled meeting with the Boss. Once again, everything along his path seemed as perfectly normal as it had days earlier. Zax loaded up a tray with everything he wanted except for his favorite pastries which were missing. If it hadn't been for his limp and the residual pain in his leg, Zax might have been convinced he had dreamed the entire civilian revolt. And then, he saw incontrovertible evidence it had all been real.

Rege was sitting with a group of the civilians who had been with him in Engineering. They were sprawled around the table with their blasters jumbled in a heap at one end. Their trays were piled high with half-eaten food. The civilians were talking boisterously, and Zax noticed how the nearby Crew had left a buffer zone of empty tables all around them.

Zax turned to head off to a different section of tables, but Rege noticed him and called out.

"Cadet Zax—a moment please."

Rege's hair wasn't greasy like it had been, but rather appeared freshly washed. It was also pulled back into a neat ponytail so it no longer fell across his eyes. He wore his brother's knife in a sheath on his belt and his hand casually rested on its hilt as he approached and spoke.

"It's amazing to see you up walking around cadet, especially knowing how hard I crushed your leg the other day. It's impressive what Crew medical treatment can do. If a civilian had been hurt like that, he'd have been crippled for months. Only the best for the Crew, though, just like all of this amazing food. My friends and I could spend every minute of the day in here for the next month stuffing our faces and still not catch up on the calorie deficits we've dealt with for the past few years. Hell, just taking the trash from some of your fellow cadets' trays would feed a civilian family for days."

The man seemed like he was trying to bait him somehow, but Zax maintained a neutral expression and stared back silently. The civilian continued.

"Well, I'd really love to chat more, but I need to finish up breakfast and get back to work. I'm leading the transition team for President Imair, and we need to figure out how to start reallocating the Ship's resources more equitably. Be sure to enjoy your breakfast as I'm guessing mealtime will start looking a little different around here soon."

Rege turned to walk back to his table but then paused and looked back. "By the way, we're going to be seeing a lot more of each other in the future. Once I'm done with the transition, Imair's promised me I can be her representative in Flight Ops. I hear that's where you're getting assigned as well now that you're done with Waste Systems. I look forward to working closely with you."

The civilian returned to his table where everyone laughed uproariously at whatever he said to them as he sat down. Zax hung his head and shuffled over to his usual spot. The excitement he felt at returning to Flight Ops was shattered at the discovery he would have to work side-by-side with the civilian responsible for Kalare's murder. He plopped down in this seat and picked halfheartedly at the food on his tray until footsteps approached from behind.

"Hey there, Zax! It's great to see you! I hoped I'd find you here. I just missed you this morning when I went to see you in medbay. I was in to see you yesterday too, but you were still sleeping. It was that same medic on duty who treated me last year. He said you'd been sleeping for thirty-six hours. It was such a weird coincidence how you were in that same bed again where I was the first time you came to visit me. Remember—after Cyrus blew out my knee? My leg was in a cast that day and you were in there yesterday with a cast on your leg! It seems crazy for someone with nothing more than a busted leg to sleep that long. I'm the one who practically died, and I was awake and moving around within twenty secs of the anesthesia wearing off. It just goes to prove yet again how girls are tougher than boys. Why are you looking at me like that?"

Zax had spun around as soon as he heard the voice, and his eyes went wide at seeing Kalare in front of him. He wanted to interrupt and ask a million questions, but she got so deep, so fast into one of her monologues that he decided to just sit back and happily wait it out. As he did so, his smile grew larger and more intense. When Kalare finally paused and allowed him to respond he could only get out one word. "How?"

She beamed and lifted her shirt to reveal a massive scar on her stomach. It was a shade of furious scarlet, but the borders were fading and it would eventually disappear.

"I got this thanks to that oxygen thief, Aleron. We had almost reached a Marine garrison when Captain Clueless stopped listening to the corporal's directions and bolted ahead of us. Of course, he ran straight into a group of civilians. The corporal had no choice but to engage them in a firefight which ended when he got shot. They took us prisoner, and we listened as their squad leader called in for orders. It took ages, but I overheard when he was finally told to kill me and Aleron and make it painful.

"The civilian didn't hesitate before shooting us both in the belly. I guess his plan was to have us bleed out slow since gut wounds are supposed to be pretty nasty. He was about to shoot the Marine in the head when the passageway lit up with blaster fire. We were close enough to the garrison that they had heard the firefight and sent Marines in ChamWare to check out what was happening. They got us back to medics pretty quickly, so here I am!"

Zax was flabbergasted. He had given Kalare up for dead when Rege first gave the order and had relived that pain so many times in the hours since. To have her show up looking and acting the same as always was almost more than his heart could bear. He was trying to figure out what to say when the screens lit up around the mess hall to show the morning newsvid. Kalare squealed with excitement.

"Ooohhh, we've got to watch this! There haven't been any broadcasts since everything happened, but I heard last night that we'd see a full report this morning about what ended the revolution and how things are going to work around here now with the civilians in charge."

She pulled up a chair and sat brushing against him. Zax wanted to do nothing but bask in the warmth of her body so close to his, but he forced himself to pay attention as the announcer spoke.

"We've got a special report for you today with the full details of what happened recently along with initial information about what you should expect to see moving forward.

"A group of brave civilians took decisive action three days ago based on concerns which have simmered this past year regarding the viability of our Mission. After evidence surfaced that additional humans are traveling the stars, these selfless individuals concluded they must influence a change in our Mission."

Zax couldn't believe his ears. The same announcer who had spent the past year bemoaning the atrocious behavior of the civilians was now describing them as heroes.

"Their goal was to avoid as much bloodshed as possible while ensuring their message was heard and acted upon by the Captain and Omegas. They only took this action after repeated attempts at peaceful discussion through normal channels had been rebuffed. Thankfully, through the calm thinking of their leaders and the eventual cooperation of a senior

member of the Crew, they were able to achieve their objectives."

A picture of the Boss appeared on the screen. He was bloodied and disheveled—the exact opposite of how he had looked right before handing over the FTL engine.

"The final resolution became possible when the Flight Boss determined he needed to step in to do what was best for everyone on the Ship—Crew and civilian alike. He was initially resistant to the requests of the civilians, as can be seen here with the physical evidence of how he withstood their augmented interrogation techniques. In an exclusive interview this morning, we learned the thought process behind how his conclusions shifted and we will air that footage later. Suffice it to say, you'll want to hear it straight from his mouth.

"What I can tell you now is that the Boss realized the Captain's intent to vent the Ship and murder ten million humans was unjust and unlawful. He halted his resistance to the civilian's requests and ultimately brokered a deal between them and the Captain. This deal included the Captain's agreement to step down, temporarily, pending a full review of her actions. The Flight Boss is now in charge of all Crew matters, albeit within a new command structure that includes much needed civilian oversight. It is this new leadership structure that we are going to discuss first, starting with this footage

from an announcement that was made earlier this morning."

Zax bolted upright. "That's entirely a lie! None of that happened like what they're saying! The Boss wasn't tortured, he didn't broker any deal, he just gave in to the civilians plain and simple and sold out the Captain in the process. All so he could save his own skin and stay in charge!"

Kalare had become alert and sat ramrod straight with the shock of Zax's sudden movement, but after listening to his outburst she leaned back, slowly shook her head, and sighed. "Not this all over again..."

If you liked reading about Zax and Kalare and would like to read more about their adventures on the Ship, send an email to Zax@theshipseries.com and ask for the first 5 chapters of Volume 3.

Acknowledgments

About three years ago I was going through some particularly khrazy times in my life. My therapist (thank you R.G!) suggested that a great way to get myself more grounded would be a creative, right-brain activity that would balance all of the left-brain work that dominates my professional life. The seeds of this story had been bouncing around in my head for a while so I decided to take the plunge and write a novel.

Me being me, I actually decided that I would not write just one novel, but a series of SEVEN. Thankfully, I managed to talk myself off that particular ledge and you are holding in your hand book two of what will be only (!) a five volume series.

There are many people who played a role in getting this book published. The first is Owen Egerton. Owen is a creative polymath of the highest order who I am fortunate enough to call a friend. The degree to which he is wildly talented is surpassed only by the generosity with which he shares his talents. I remember how terrified I was the first time I talked to Owen about this project. He could have easily patted me on the head and said "nice try, kid", but instead he gave not only warm encouragement but also invaluable advice.

I was also lucky to benefit from my friendship with the other half of the talented Egerton duo when Jodi became my first editor. I'm tempted to go back and read some of the early drafts to see how far the story (and the prose) has come in that time, but I'm not sure I really want to subject myself to that kind of abuse. Jodi gave fantastic guidance and support when this project teetered between an absolute lark and something I really wanted to pour my heart into. Her encouragement pushed it forward into the form it is today.

Jodi eventually handed me off to a new editor in Stacey Swann. Stacey's guidance has absolutely made a huge difference in where this book wound up–both from a plot perspective as well as the writing style and quality. Her contributions were endless and will be eternally appreciated.

Outside of the professionals, I also benefited tremendously from the input of early readers among my friends. Kathleen Trail gave a couple of gentle pointers in the very early going that stuck with me throughout. Michael Lee was not only willing to read multiple drafts, he was also tremendously supportive and encouraging throughout the entire process. I will state here for the record that his life debt owed to me is discharged in light of his service to the Ship.

As the story got more and more refined, I was brave enough to share it with a larger group of friends who all provided encouragement and feedback. Huge appreciation for Laura Parrot Perry, Amy Nylund, Clayton and Tisha Havens, Scherry Sweeney, Scott Hyman, and Zachary W. All of those folks took the time to read and provide some great input.

Many thanks to Bryan McNeal for the cover concepts and art. I am honored that my book and Gatti's Pizza have both benefited from Bryan's artistry.

Finally, I want to express tremendous gratitude for my family. My lovely wife Kerry has provided constant encouragement and exhibited fantastic restraint about the number of Saturday and Sunday mornings I've spent typing away at Starbucks. My eldest, Parker, was super enthusiastic about reading the very first draft of volume one, even though he probably should have been begging me to refine it before unleashing it upon him. My youngest, Wesley, had book one read aloud by Kerry, and still managed to remember it a year later when I read volume two to him. The whole family provided great feedback and inspiration—even if Kerry still rants about the pronunciation of Kalare's name.